HALL OF MIRRORS

KATHY LEE

© Kathy Lee 2011
First published 2011
ISBN 978 1 84427 506 9

Scripture Union
207–209 Queensway, Bletchley, Milton Keynes, MK2 2EB
Email: info@scriptureunion.org.uk
Website: www.scriptureunion.org.uk

Scripture Union Australia
Locked Bag 2, Central Coast Business Centre, NSW 2252
Website: www.scriptureunion.org.au

Scripture Union USA
PO Box 987, Valley Forge, PA 19482
Website: www.scriptureunion.org

British Library Cataloguing-in-Publication Data
A catalogue record of this book is available from the British Library.

Printed and bound by Nutech Print Services, India.

Cover design: Dodo Mammoth Reindeer Fox

🐚 Scripture Union is an international charity working with churches in more than 130 countries, providing resources to bring the good news of Jesus Christ to children, young people and families and to encourage them to develop spiritually through the Bible and prayer.

As well as our network of volunteers, staff and associates who run holidays, church-based events and school Christian groups, we produce a wide range of publications and support those who use our resources through training programmes.

Chapter 1:

Face of a ghost?

Mallenford Hall used to frighten me when I was little. It loomed up at the far end of the drive, a vast, grey building, with dozens of tall windows that seemed to stare at me. It didn't look like a home where people could live and be happy. It looked more like a museum, or a prison.

It was even more scary inside. The rooms were enormous, high and echoing. The light was dim because most of the blinds were down. The furniture was old, grand and faded. On the walls were gloomy pictures of people from long ago; some of them had probably died in the place. There were rumours that it was haunted.

I think it was the silence and emptiness that frightened me. There was nobody actually living there. The owner, Miss Morton, lived in London; it was several years since she'd been to visit Mallenford Hall. People said she disliked the place, but didn't want to sell it.

When the first Earl of Mallenford built the Hall, 250 years ago, servants were cheap. There would have been plenty of people around then – kitchen maids and housemaids, footmen, gardeners, a butler and a cook.

Now there was no one but us. My dad was the one and only gardener, struggling to keep the huge gardens from turning into a jungle. My mum was the housekeeper. She cleaned and dusted and aired the place, which was all rather pointless, I thought. Nobody ever went there, except for the one weekend a year when the Hall was open to the public, raising money for charity.

We lived in a small cottage called the Lodge. It was right next to the main gates of the Hall.

"In the old days," Mum told me, "there would have been a lodge-keeper living here. His job was to open and shut the gates whenever a carriage arrived. Electronic gates hadn't been invented."

"He probably had a wife and six kids living in this house," Dad said. "They had big families in those days. So don't complain about not having enough space, Rebecca."

I didn't complain because I was used to it. I couldn't remember living anywhere else. But it was a very small house. The kitchen was the size of a cupboard. My bedroom, up in the roof, had walls that sloped inwards like a tent.

It was silly, in a way, having all those empty rooms at the Hall, when we were crammed into a house the size of a hamster cage. But I never wanted to live in such gloomy, depressing splendour. I wouldn't have liked a huge bedroom with heavy velvet curtains. I preferred my little attic room, where at night I could listen to the trees whispering and the owls calling.

The Hall was two miles outside the town of Mallenford, where I went to school. We didn't have any near neighbours, and this made it harder to find friends. On the school bus, by the time it reached me, people from the distant villages had formed their own little groups. I often had to sit on my own.

All through junior school I had a good friend called Sarah, who went to the same Sunday Meetings as my family. But just before we started senior school, her family moved away. Mallenford High School was quite big – 150 kids in each year. You'd think that somewhere in that crowd, I would have been able to find a friend. But it wasn't easy.

Part of the problem was the strict rules of the Sunday Meeting. The rules didn't allow us to have a TV at home, or a computer, or even a radio. So, when people talked about the latest TV show, I had no idea what they were on about. They mentioned things like online chatrooms – I hardly knew what that meant.

When you can't join in with what people are talking about, they think you're either very shy or very stupid. It was obvious that I wasn't stupid because I was good at most of my school subjects. So people assumed I was shy.

After a while they stopped trying to include me in conversations. I was lucky; I didn't get bullied, just ignored. When teams were picked, I would be one of the last ones chosen. I was never invited to parties, which didn't really matter, because Dad wouldn't have let me go. But it would have been nice to be asked.

At lunchtimes, having nobody to hang around with, I usually went to the school library. I read all kinds of books, but fantasies were my favourite. I could lose myself for a while in a land of dragons, magic castles and perilous journeys. Then the bell would ring for afternoon lessons, like an evil spell destroying my secret world.

In the library there were several computers, although I never used them. I wasn't supposed to go near them, and I hadn't told Dad that we sometimes had to use computers in lessons. When I had to do that, I was so slow that I annoyed other people. "Rebecca's got the keyboard skills of a gorilla," I heard somebody say once.

One day, when I finished a library book and went to get another one, I happened to glance at a computer screen. There was a photo that I recognised instantly. It was the Hall, seen from outside the gates.

I must have let out a gasp of surprise, or something, because the person using the computer turned his head. It was Dylan, a boy from my class.

"Something the matter?" he said to me.

"That's Mallenford Hall, isn't it?" I said.

"Yeah. Have you ever been there?"

"Oh yes. I live there."

"You live at Mallenford Hall?" Suddenly he looked very interested.

"Well, not exactly in the Hall. In the Lodge at the gates. My parents work at the Hall."

"Have you actually been inside?"

"Yes, of course. Lots of times."

He lowered his voice. "Ever seen the ghost?"

Oh-oh. I should have known he wasn't really interested in *me*. Everybody knew that Dylan was obsessed with ghosts and vampires and supernatural stuff. When he brought up the subject in lessons, people would groan with boredom.

I said, "Which ghost?" because there were several, if you believed old Mrs Dawkins, who used to come in and help my mum at spring-cleaning time. She said there was a headless coachman driving four black horses, and a ghostly monk, and a young girl who killed herself by jumping from an attic window. (Mum said it was all nonsense. She didn't believe in ghosts.)

"This one," said Dylan.

He pressed a button, changing the picture on the screen. Now there was a close-up of the top-floor windows of the Hall. The window panes looked quite dark, except for a pale, oval shape at the side of one of them. If you used your imagination, it might be a face... or it might be just the reflection of light on the window.

"Do you know which room that is?" Dylan asked me.

"Not exactly. The top floor is never used nowadays. There's a long corridor with a row of locked doors – it must be one of those rooms."

"So it's true what it says on the website," said Dylan. "*The window in the photograph belongs to a room which is believed to have been locked up for years.* So that's not a human face. It must be a ghost."

"Wait a minute," I said. "Who took that photo? How did they get in?"

Dylan read some more. "*This photo was taken on 5 September last year. Mallenford Hall is only open on one weekend a year, access strictly limited to the gardens and the lower floors of the building. When I tried to arrange another visit last autumn, the housekeeper was not exactly helpful! She told me I would have to write to the owner for permission, but would not reveal the owner's address.*"

"That's my mum," I said. "She's the housekeeper. She wouldn't want to be bothered with people coming round whenever they feel like it."

If Mum had her way, the Hall would never be open for viewing. The open weekend was just a nuisance. "But I suppose it's in a good cause," she would say, and sigh deeply.

Dylan said, "So if I want to have a closer look at the Hall, I have to wait until it's open in September? That's ages away. I was hoping I might be able to see it sooner than that."

"You can see it all right," I said. "From outside the gates."

I could sense his disappointment. He wasn't one of the boys that girls in my class went mad about – he was too odd, too different. All the same, he wasn't bad-looking, I thought. He had a dark fringe of hair and deep, mysterious eyes. And those eyes had a pleading look which was hard to ignore.

"I don't suppose you could ask your mum to let me just have a quick look? Half an hour, that's all. I promise I wouldn't cause any trouble."

"Well, I can ask her," I said. "But don't get your hopes up."

Chapter 2:

Mirrors

Mum surprised me – she must have been in a good mood. She said Dylan could come and look round the Hall after school one day. (I had told her he was interested in history, which was perfectly true. Ghost stories all begin sometime in the past, after all.)

"But he can't go wandering around on his own," she said. "There are too many valuable things on display. If any of them were to go missing, I'd be in real trouble."

"I can keep an eye on him," I said.

"You won't have to. I'll give him a guided tour," said Mum.

"Oh." That wasn't what Dylan wanted, but it would be better than nothing. "And can he take some photos?"

"I don't see why not."

Dylan arrived by bike. I was waiting for him. I opened the little gate at the side of the big double entrance gates. He wheeled his bike through and put it by our back door, all the time staring along the drive at the Hall.

"Big, isn't it?" I said.

"Huge. How many rooms are there?"

"I'm not sure. There are 18 bedrooms, not counting the servants' rooms in the attic. My mum's going to show you round."

Mum surprised me again by asking Dylan if he would like a drink. He must be thirsty after his bike ride.

"Yes please," said Dylan.

It felt odd to see him in our living-room. I had never had a friend round since Sarah moved away, nearly a year ago. And Dylan wasn't really a friend. He hadn't come to see me – he had come to look for ghosts.

But Mum didn't know that. She expected me to go along with my new best friend as she showed him around the Hall. So I went, although of course I'd seen it all before.

Walking up the drive, I looked up at the top-floor windows. There was no sign of a face at any of them. They seemed as dark as caves, with no light reflected from the glass. But then, it was a dull, cloudy day – things might have been different when that picture was taken.

Although there was nothing to see, Dylan stopped to take a photo. "You never know," he muttered to me. "Sometimes things don't show up until the picture goes onto the computer."

Mum led us through the vast, echoing rooms on the ground floor – the Blue Room, the dining room, the Chinese room, the library, the Yellow Room, the music room. Dylan tried to look interested.

"Of course, these interiors aren't as old as the house itself," Mum said in her tour-guide voice. "Most of them were refurbished in the 1920s, when the Morton family bought the house, after the last Earl of Mallenford died."

"What happened to the last Earl?" Dylan asked.

"People said he lost his mind after his three sons were killed in the First World War. Nowadays they'd probably say he had Alzheimer's, or had a breakdown – I don't know. Anyway, he died, and there was nobody to inherit what he owned, so it went to the Crown – that means to the king of England. The strange thing is, the Earl had been a rich man, but when he died, his bank accounts were almost empty. Ever since, there have been rumours that the Mallenford fortune is hidden somewhere in the Hall or the grounds."

"Hidden treasure?" said Dylan.

"Yes. But lots of people have looked for it over the years, without finding anything."

"I tried to find it myself when I was little," I told Dylan. "I used to dig holes in the garden, looking for it."

"If the old Earl did bury anything valuable, he wouldn't have chosen the garden of the Lodge to do it in," said Mum.

"I know that now. Why didn't you tell me at the time?" I said.

"Well, it kept you happy," she said. "It got you out in the fresh air, away from your books. Always reading, our Rebecca, even at the age of seven."

"If you'd found the treasure, what would you have done with it?" Dylan asked me.

"Probably bought more books," I said, and he laughed.

It was strange. I didn't feel shy with Dylan, although boys usually made me nervous. Perhaps it was because he was on his own, not one of a big group. Or because he was a bit of an oddity – like me.

We went up the grand staircase and looked at some of the first floor bedrooms. These were not the rooms Dylan wanted to see, but he was good at asking polite questions. Up another floor, we came to the Hall of Mirrors. This time Dylan gave a gasp of amazement, as most people did when they first saw it.

It was a long, narrow room, with 11 tall windows on one side, and an equal number of arch-topped mirrors on the other side. The high vaulted ceiling was covered in paintings. There were glass chandeliers, marble panels and gilded statues. It looked very grand, although really it was just a corridor with bedrooms leading off one side of it. Some of the mirrors were actually doors, with cut-glass handles.

"This room was inspired by the famous Hall of Mirrors at the Palace of Versailles, in France," Mum said. "Of course, it's much smaller than the original. This is the oldest part of the house interior – luckily they didn't touch this room when they refurbished the ground floor."

The room was spectacular, but I had never liked it. The mirrors were so old that the glass was all spotted and marked. When you looked into them, your face was warped and twisted, with dim, brown colours like an ancient photograph.

When I was just a kid, Mum sometimes took me to Mallenford Hall with her. In the school holidays she still had her cleaning to do, but I was too young to be left at home on my own. I would sit in a corner with a book, while Mum used the big floor-polishing machine, or flicked a duster around.

If she was working in the Hall of Mirrors, I would never stay there. There was something about the place that made me uneasy. When you walked around it, you had a mirror-image companion who came and went... a warped, twisted, dim and faded copy of yourself. And your footsteps echoed as if someone was following you.

I used to sit on the cold marble floor of the landing rather than on a chair in the Hall of Mirrors. Mum would tell me I was being silly. But I could never concentrate on my reading when I was close to those mirrors. Other mirrors kept popping into my mind. Mirrors in stories are often quite strange – have you noticed? There's the stepmother's mirror in *Snow White*, the magic looking-glass that Alice stepped through, the mirror in the magician's house in Narnia, the Mirror of Erised at Hogwarts...

But Dylan didn't care about mirrors. He wasn't all that interested in the bedrooms behind the doors, either.

"This is the second floor, isn't it?" he said to Mum. "So there must be another floor up above?"

"Yes, but there's nothing much to see," said Mum. "Little rooms where the servants used to sleep in the old days – that's all there is up there."

"Oh," said Dylan. "Couldn't I just have a quick glance?"

"I suppose so," said Mum.

The grand staircase didn't go any higher, but there was another, much smaller stairway at the far end of the Hall of Mirrors. At the top was a long, narrow corridor, where the only light came from cobwebbed windows in the roof. The walls were painted a gloomy shade of dark green. There were a dozen doors, all closed.

"We hardly ever come up here," said Mum. "These doors are kept locked, but I have a key somewhere."

She had about 20 heavy keys on a key-ring as big as a plate. After several attempts, she managed to unlock one of the doors.

This room was completely different from the splendour downstairs. There was no furniture. The air smelt musty, and the bare floorboards sounded hollow underfoot.

"It's all a bit dusty, I'm afraid," said Mum. "Our spring-cleaning doesn't reach as far as this."

I looked around the empty room. "Didn't the servants have beds to sleep in?"

"Well, of course they would have had beds," Mum said. "But it must have been cold up here in winter. No fireplace. No heating at all."

"People talk about the good old days," Dylan said, taking a photo. "But they were only good if you were one of the rich people."

"That's true," said Mum. "Now, have you seen all you want to see?"

Dylan had gone over to the window. I guessed he was trying to work out if this was where the "ghostly face" had been photographed. It had been the third or fourth window from the left, I thought. But without opening the window and leaning out, it was impossible to tell if this was the one.

"Could we look at the next room as well?" he asked.

"It's exactly the same as this one," Mum said. But when he gave her that pleading look of his, she said, "Oh, all right."

As she'd said, the next room was just the same, except for a cracked chamber-pot in the corner. Dylan took a photo of the room, and then another showing the view from the window.

"We're quite high up here, aren't we?" he said. "And no bars at the window or anything."

I said, "Mrs Dawkins says that a servant girl jumped from one of these windows. She was in love with one of the Mallenford family, but he got killed in the First

World War. When the news of his death came, she killed herself."

"Have you ever heard that her ghost might haunt this place?" Dylan asked Mum.

"Oh, people say all kinds of silly things," Mum said. "But I've been working here for eight years, and I've never seen a ghost. I don't believe in them. And now, if you don't mind, I'm going to lock up again. Ready?"

Chapter 3:
Worldly things

I took Dylan outside while Mum reset the burglar alarm and locked the two heavy doors. She never liked anyone to watch her setting the alarm – even I didn't know what the code was.

"I'd like to see the gardens," Dylan said to me. "Would you be allowed to show me around?"

I had thought about suggesting that, but had chickened out. He might not want to. He might think I was after him... I was embarrassed at the very idea.

"I'd better ask Mum," I said, but Mum was quite happy for me to take Dylan around the grounds.

"That's because there's nothing valuable to steal," I explained to him. "Apart from the marble statues on the terrace, and they weigh about a ton each."

He said, "Yeah. I might have trouble nicking one of those."

"You certainly would if you tried to do it by bike." The thought made me smile... Dylan cycling through Mallenford with a six-foot-high Greek statue on his handlebars.

He gave me a curious glance.

"Why are you so quiet all the time in school, Rebecca?" he asked me. "I always thought you were... I don't know... incredibly shy. Afraid to say a word. But now I can see you're not really like that."

"I am like that in school," I said. "It's different at home."

"Why? What are you afraid of?"

It was hard to explain. I wasn't afraid exactly. I said, "I don't like it when I say something and everybody stares at me."

"They only do that because they're so surprised at you saying anything at all."

"It's like I'm a different person at school," I said. "Everybody expects me to be quiet, and so I am."

People's eyes are like mirrors, I sometimes think. You see your own reflection in them – or rather, you see what people think of you. If everyone has an image of you that shows you as quiet and shy, it's not easy to change. You can't break away from the image.

I said, "It's hard to go against what people expect you to be."

"Is it? I don't think so," Dylan said. "I say what I like to anybody about anything."

"But everybody knows you're a bit weird. Here comes Dylan... expect the unexpected. So you're doing it too. You are being like what people think you're like."

"Very clever," he said, and laughed.

We walked round the grounds of the Hall. I showed him the formal gardens near the house, where Dad kept the lawns smooth and the hedges clipped. By the pond, where the reeds grew six feet tall, nature was starting to take over. We went up the hill into the part I called the

Wild Wood, which was a total jungle. I took him to the badger's sett, a big hole with mounds of earth outside. (The badgers were having an extension done, Dad said.)

But Dylan wasn't all that interested in nature study. He pointed to a grey stone tower that rose between the trees.

"What's that thing?" he said.

"That's the Folly. It looks like an old ruined castle, but it's not real. One of the Earls had it built in seventeen hundred and something, I think. Want to see it?"

The Folly stood in a clearing of the wood. There was a wide, grassy path leading to it, so that it could be seen from the Hall. It had broken-down walls and a tower with crumbling battlements on top.

"It was built like this," I said. "Built as a ruin, I mean. It was supposed to look picturesque."

"I don't suppose it's haunted, then?" he said.

"Oh yes. It is. The Earl paid an old man to live here and pretend to be a hermit. But he got ill and died, and nobody found his body for ages. I mean, a hermit – they're supposed to keep away from people. His ghost is said to haunt the Folly. But nobody's ever seen it or heard it."

"If nobody's seen or heard the ghost, how do they know... Hey, wait a minute. You just made that up!"

I grinned at him, but he didn't smile back. I saw that the ghost thing wasn't a joke to him – it was quite serious. Deadly serious, you might say.

I said, "All right, so I made that up. But I didn't make up what Mrs Dawkins said about the girl who jumped out of the window. Maybe she was the ghostly face in the photo."

"Do you know anything more about her?" he said eagerly.

"No. I don't even know her name."

"I must look this up," said Dylan. "Do you know when it happened?"

"Well, sometime during the First World War. Nearly a hundred years ago. Just about everybody who was alive then must be dead by now."

"I bet I can still find some mention of it on the internet," said Dylan. "Everything in the entire world is on the internet. And then there's the hidden treasure, the lost fortune of the Mallenfords. Sounds mysterious… I like mysteries."

We went back to the Lodge, where Dylan had left his bike. He wanted to thank my mum for letting him look at the Hall, so I took him indoors. I had forgotten that it was nearly tea-time, and Dad might have finished work.

Dad didn't look pleased when he saw Dylan come in. He gave me a long stare that meant there would be trouble later. But he said nothing while Dylan was there.

Mum looked worried. She got the food on the table quickly. Dad was always hungry after working outside all day. I knew what she was thinking... he would be in a better mood when he'd eaten.

Dad said a prayer to give thanks for the meal. Then, without even taking a bite, he said, "Who was that boy, Rebecca?"

"Just somebody from my class at school," I said. "He wanted to look at the Hall."

"Why did you let him come into our house?"

"He wanted to say thank you to Mum for showing him around," I said.

"There was no need to bring him indoors," Dad said sternly. "He could have talked to your mother at the door."

I looked towards Mum for help. She had actually been the one who invited Dylan in, when he first arrived and she gave him a drink. But I didn't want to get Mum into trouble too, so I kept quiet.

Mum said, "He seemed like a nice boy. Very polite."

Dad's voice was sharp. "I don't care how nice he seems – he's not one of us. We are to be apart from all unbelievers. We must keep ourselves pure and undefiled by the world. You must have heard me say it hundreds of times!"

I nodded.

"So don't have him back here. Do you understand me?"

"Yes," I whispered.

I told myself that it didn't matter. Dylan probably wouldn't want to come back here, anyway. He would find some other mystery or ghost story on his computer, and go off in a completely different direction.

Dad turned his attention to Mum. "I don't know what you were thinking about, encouraging this friendship."

"I just thought it might be a good thing for Rebecca," Mum said. "Ever since Sarah's family moved away, she's seemed... well, a bit lonely."

"It's far better to be alone than to mingle with worldly people," Dad said. *"Come out from the midst of them, and be separated, saith the Lord."*

Mum didn't argue. It never did any good to argue with Dad. He knew the Bible inside out, and he had an answer for everything.

I thought Mum looked rather sad. I realised then that I might not be the only one who was feeling lonely. Mum had friends at the Meeting, of course. But that was in Yanderton, five miles away.

Evenings were quiet in our house. Nobody ever came to call. Mum would get her sewing out; Dad would study the Bible. On summer evenings Dad sometimes took me walking in Deepdene Woods, where we might see deer and foxes. In winter I stayed indoors, reading or doing my homework.

What would it be like if we didn't belong to the Meeting? Surely life would be more interesting. We'd have a TV and a thing to play music and films on. (I had never seen a film apart from educational ones, in school.) And I might have my own phone to talk to my friends. If I had any friends.

But all those things were said to be evil and worldly. They corrupted you. You shouldn't even think about wanting them. God, who knew the thoughts of every heart, would know I was wondering about those forbidden things. I was sure he would be angry with me, even angrier than my father.

I pushed the thoughts away from me. I got my homework books out with a sigh.

Chapter 4:

The new girl

On Sunday, when we went to the Meeting, there was a new family there. They had five children; the biggest one was a girl who looked about my age. Afterwards, one of the Elders introduced them to us. Their name was Fairweather, and they had come to live in Mallenford. The girl called Lois would be going to my school.

I was pleased. Lois might not turn out to be a good friend, like Sarah used to be. But at least she would understand my life. She would know why I couldn't talk about pop music and fashion and things.

Lois had long hair, of course. All women and girls at the Meeting had long hair, tied back with a headscarf whenever they went out. She had brown eyes and a face full of freckles. She looked me over carefully, without smiling.

What was she seeing? A mirror image of herself? My own hair was fair and my eyes were grey, but apart from that we looked quite similar. We were both wearing the kind of clothes required for the Meeting... long skirts, high-necked tops, and headscarves, of course. It was like a uniform. You had to wear it, whether it suited you or not.

"How old are you?" Lois asked me.

"Twelve."

"Me too. We might be in the same class."

"We'll definitely be in the same year," I said. "But there are five separate classes in Year 7, so you might be in a different one. When are you starting?"

"Tomorrow."

"It's only 3 weeks to the end of term," I said. "Hardly worth starting."

"I know," said Lois. "I tried to tell Dad that. But you know what fathers are like."

I looked over to where her father was talking to mine. They looked alike, too, in the usual men's clothing, white shirts and dark trousers. They seemed to be getting on all right. Lois's mum was talking non-stop to my mum, who was listening without getting a word in edgeways.

"And Rebecca must come over after school to play with Lois," Mrs Fairweather was saying. "We'd love to have her."

Play with Lois? How old did she think we were – eight?

"How nice," Mum said. "I'm sure Rebecca will look forward to that."

Next day, in school, I kept an eye out for Lois. I saw her at lunchtime. She'd been put in a different form from me, and she didn't like her form teacher.

"He told me I couldn't wear my headscarf because it was against school rules. My dad will have something to say about that! They let Muslim girls wear their scarves, so they can't stop us wearing ours. Why aren't you wearing yours?" She gave me an accusing stare.

Actually I had been quite glad that school rules didn't let me wear my headscarf during school hours. I didn't like wearing it. It was just one more thing that marked me out as different from everyone else.

If Lois got permission to wear a headscarf in school, would I have to wear mine too? I really hoped not. But Dad would expect me to do it, if Lois did.

We ate our packed lunches together at our own little table in the dining-room. (I was used to sitting there by myself, because the Meeting rules didn't allow eating at the same table with unbelievers.) Afterwards I took Lois on a tour of the school. We ended up in my usual refuge, the library.

That was a mistake, because Dylan was in there. He was at a computer with another boy. When he saw me, he called out, "Hey, Rebecca! Have a look at this!"

He was pointing to something on the screen. But I couldn't look at it – not with Lois's beady eye on me. She would probably tell her dad I had been using a computer, and her dad would tell my dad... big trouble.

"I can't," I said, feeling awkward. "This is Lois – she's a new girl. I'm just showing her around the school."

We made a hasty exit. I dragged Lois round some more sights of the school, but I was running out of ideas.

"This is the office. And that's the medical room over there. Oh, and the caretaker's place. Don't ever go there."

"Why not?"

"Because the caretaker hates all school kids. It's funny about school caretakers. They always seem to hate children. I can't think why."

"Maybe it's because they have to clear up the mess that some people make," Lois explained to me, as if I was an idiot.

I felt relieved when the bell rang and we had to go to our separate lessons.

The History teacher, who lived in a different time frame from everyone else, was often late. As we waited for him to arrive, Dylan passed me a sheet of paper. It looked as if he had printed it from the computer.

UNSOLVED MYSTERIES: THE MALLENFORD MILLIONS

The strange disappearance of the seventh Earl of Mallenford has never been explained. In 1919, at the end of World War One – the war in which his three sons lost their lives – he vanished from London society. At first it was assumed that he had gone to his country house, Mallenford Hall. He was known to have been overcome with grief at the loss of all three of his children.

Mallenford Hall, at this time, was deserted. Most of the staff had been called up into the army or the ammunition factories. In 1916 the building had been turned into a hospital for wounded soldiers. After the fighting ceased, it was no longer needed, and the Hall lay empty.

The Earl (then aged 62) was not to be found at the Hall, or his Mayfair house, or his Scottish shooting-lodge. There was no record of his leaving the country. He seemed to have completely disappeared. And something else had vanished too: a large sum of money - £50,000 (equivalent to over £2,000,000 in today's currency.)

It was his own money. He had withdrawn it from his various bank accounts, which he had a perfect right to do. The mystery was why he should need such a huge sum of money. What had he done with it, and why had he disappeared? Had some terrible crime – blackmail or murder – been committed?

His friends reported him missing. The police made enquiries. Advertisements were placed in national newspapers, without result. The Earl of Mallenford appeared to have vanished off the face of the earth.

Several months later, police in a Lancashire village arrested an old tramp who was acting strangely. At first he was thought to be drunk, but when he failed to sober up, he was taken to the Insane Asylum at Lancaster. Here, a doctor identified him from his photographs in the paper and a distinctive birthmark on his shoulder. The missing Earl had been found.

But he was now quite senile. His memory had completely gone; he could not answer any questions about where he had been since his disappearance. He lived out the last few months of his life in a private clinic, where he seemed to be fairly happy. He had forgotten his grief over his sons, forgotten who he was… forgotten everything.

As for the money, what he did with it has never been discovered. Perhaps he gave it away; perhaps it was stolen from him; perhaps he lost it, or buried it. (Rumours persist that it is hidden somewhere in Mallenford Hall, either in the house or the grounds.)

The people named in his will, his wife and three sons, were all dead; there were no other relatives to inherit his property or title. The Earldom of Mallenford became extinct. Mallenford Hall was later bought by Thomas Morton, a steel manufacturer who had made a fortune during the war. He carried out major changes to the building, but never found the missing money.

"Well!" I said. "So Mrs Dawkins was right. Maybe there is a hidden treasure."

"If there is," said Dylan, "I'm going to find it."

Chapter 5:
So long ago

"A pigeon's come down the chimney in the Yellow Room," Mum said. "It's made a terrible mess – there's soot everywhere. I'll have to get Mrs Dawkins in to help clean up."

"I could help," I offered. I wanted to talk to Mrs Dawkins – I had promised Dylan that I would try and find out some more about the Hall and its mysterious past.

"There might be a secret room somewhere in the building," Dylan had said. "Could be, only the Earl and his sons knew about it, and now the secret has been lost."

"I don't think so. A secret room would have been found when the Morton family refurbished the place in the 1920s."

Dylan said, "Not if it was upstairs. Didn't your mum say that the Hall of Mirrors had never been done up? Same with the top floor, by the look of things."

A secret room... how would you find it? I thought of Sherlock Holmes stories I had read. It was always a give-away if the outside of a house didn't quite match the inside – rooms too small or corridors too short. But Mallenford Hall was so vast, how on earth could you measure it?

On Saturday, I helped Mum and Mrs Dawkins clean up the Yellow Room. There were sooty marks all over the walls, where the trapped bird had flown around desperately, trying to get out. A grey, bird-shaped imprint was on the window-pane.

"What happened to the bird?" I asked Mum. "Did it die?"

"No. I opened the window and it flew out," said Mum. "But what a mess it's made! I think I'd better tell Miss Morton that the whole room needs repainting. We can't have it like this for the Open Day."

I felt quite sorry for the bird, trapped in this room. It had flown round and round, getting nowhere, exhausting itself. And then, suddenly, the open window and freedom! At the thought, my heart leaped.

Sometimes I felt trapped too. I felt walled in by all the rules of the Meeting. Don't do this – don't do that. Avoid those people at all costs. Read the Bible and pray every day. Go to three meetings each Sunday, and never miss the prayer meetings during the week.

It was all meant to bring us closer to God, but for me, it was doing the opposite. I was bored and fed up with all of it. I wished I could stop belonging to the Meeting – but the only way to do that would be to leave home. Maybe when I got older...

I rubbed away at a wall mirror, polishing off the soot. My own reflection was doing the same thing in reverse. That girl in the mirror, who looked exactly like me, was trapped too. She could never escape from behind the glass.

Did she want to get out of there, or was she perfectly happy? Where did she go to when I walked away from the mirror?

"Wake up, love." Mrs Dawkins gave my arm a little shake. "I was just saying, how's about you putting the kettle on and making me a nice cup of tea?"

"All right. Do you want one, Mum?"

"No thanks. I'll have one later."

I put the kettle on. Apart from when we made the odd cup of tea, the vast kitchen was never used these days. There was a huge iron cooking range, which must have been ultra-modern in the 1920s, and an ancient fridge, massive on the outside, but tiny inside. (Maybe there was a secret room inside the fridge?)

Mrs Dawkins came in and sat herself down at the long wooden table. "Oh, my legs," she said. "I'm getting too old for this lark."

I asked her how old she was, but she wouldn't tell me. "I'm as old as my tongue and a bit older than my teeth. That's what my old Nan always used to say."

"Your Nan used to work at the Hall, didn't she?" I knew about this because Mrs Dawkins had mentioned it before. In fact, she talked about it every time she came here. "When would that have been?"

"Oh, in the good old days, as she called them, before the First World War. Left school at 12, my Nan did –

that's what a lot of girls had to do, and most of them went into service. There wasn't much choice for girls in them days. Anyway, she was lucky, she got took on as a maid here at the Hall. She saw the King once, when he came to visit."

"Did your Nan ever say anything about a secret room here?"

"No. I don't think so. I mean, there's always been talk about a secret passage between the Hall and the Folly, but that's just daft. Why would anyone want to dig a tunnel to that old ruin?"

"To hide something, maybe," I said.

"Ah, you're thinking about the old Earl and his money, aren't you, girl? My Nan used to say he'd probably thrown it in the river. All his money hadn't brought him any happiness. It couldn't make up to him for losing his sons."

"Was your Nan here when that servant girl killed herself?" I asked.

"Yes. That was a sad business. My Nan said the girl was in love with Master Frank, the eldest son of the family. And he loved her too, that was the pity of it, but the old Earl would never have let him marry her. The son of an Earl was supposed to marry a well-brought-up girl from a County family. Terrible snobs people were in them days."

"What was the girl's name?" I asked.

"Let me see now. I think it was Lorna… that's right… Lorna Marshall. She was a lovely girl, Nan said. They were friends, and Lorna told Nan a secret – Master Frank wanted to marry her. But they might have to marry secretly, or maybe run away to Scotland. The laws were different up there. You could get married at 16 without anybody's permission."

"So she was only 16? How old was Frank?"

"He was a bit older, 22 or 23 when the war began. He was in the army. He went off to France, to fight in the trenches, and within a few months he was dead. And Lorna, when the news came, ran upstairs and locked herself in the bedroom. My Nan tried to get her to come out. But Lorna was in floods of tears and wouldn't listen."

"Oh, how awful."

"Nan heard her banging about, as if she was trying to find something. She heard the bed being dragged across the floor. And then Lorna cried out, *It's gone! They've taken it!* What she meant, Nan had no idea. But then she heard the window being opened. Nan shouted for help, and they broke the door down, but too late.

"The worst of it was…" Mrs Dawkins lowered her voice, although the room was empty. "My Nan thought Lorna was expecting a baby. And that was a terrible thing in them days – to have a baby without being married. You would get thrown out of your job. Nobody would want to know you, not even your own family. You'd probably end up on the streets."

"But surely if she had told somebody… I mean, her baby would have been the Earl's grandchild!"

"Oh, the old Earl would have shown her the door straight away. He wouldn't have wanted anyone to know that his son had got a servant girl in the family way. Not him. He was a stickler for doing things right and proper."

"It's all so sad," I said.

"Yes. But it's a long time ago. Water under the bridge – gone and forgotten."

I had to ask her one more thing. "Did your Nan ever say anything about seeing Lorna's ghost?"

"A few people thought they saw and heard things. A shadow moving in the upstairs corridor, a board creaking in an empty room… And nobody wanted to sleep in that bedroom, the one she jumped out of, after a kitchen maid kept dreaming about her. Lorna was looking for something, the girl said – looking and looking, but she couldn't find it."

"Which bedroom was it?"

"I don't know, girl." She swilled down the last of her tea. "And now we'd better get back to work. Don't want your mum to think we've gone on strike, do we?"

Chapter 6:
Sinful

Lois Fairweather was turning out to be a real nuisance. Her father went to see the head teacher, saying it was important for religious reasons that we should cover our hair. And he told my dad what he had done. I had expected that – people in the Meeting were always comparing notes, checking up on one another.

Dad was furious when he found out I hadn't been wearing my headscarf during school hours. He hadn't realised, because I always put it on as I left in the morning and before I came home.

"Why didn't you tell me you weren't being allowed to cover your head at school?" he said sternly.

"I… I didn't think it was important," I muttered.

"Of course it's important! *Every woman praying or prophesying with her head uncovered puts her own head to shame.*"

I wanted to say, I'm not praying or prophesying when I'm at school! But it wasn't a good idea to argue with Dad when he was angry.

"Just make sure you never forget your headscarf from now on," Dad said. "Don't make me ashamed of you."

So I had one more thing that made me feel like an odd-one-out at school. One more reason to hide away from attention.

I wanted to tell Dylan what I'd found out, but several days went by without the chance to talk to him, because Lois was always hanging around. I couldn't even enjoy my lunchtime reading sessions in the library. Lois, who wasn't interested in books, kept on talking. I knew that if I told her to get lost, my parents would get to hear about it, and Dad would be angry.

On Friday, she didn't show up at school. She must be ill. Great!

I hurried to the library at lunchtime, hoping Dylan would be there. He was at the computer, as usual. Another boy was there too, someone I didn't know. He had wild red hair that needed cutting. It didn't go with his serious-looking face.

"This is Luke," Dylan said to me. "He's helping with the treasure hunt thing. Did you find out anything new?"

"Not about the treasure. But I did find out some more about the haunting." I told him everything Mrs Dawkins had said.

"So maybe that face at the window was Lorna's ghost!" said Dylan. "And she seemed to be looking for something... what could it be?"

"It can't have been the treasure," I said. "This was at the start of the War, several years before the Earl and his money disappeared."

Luke said, "Forget the ghost. I don't think it has anything to do with the missing money. It probably doesn't exist, anyway."

"Luke doesn't believe in ghosts," Dylan said.

"I don't either," I said. "At least, I didn't... now I'm not so sure."

"I would really like to have another look around inside the Hall," said Dylan. "That's the most likely place for the Earl to hide his money. I'd like to look again at that Hall of Mirrors. It's just the sort of place where there might be a hidden door. Press the right spot on one of the carvings, and the secret panel swings open... and there it is, the Earl of Mallenford's hoard of gold."

"What is this Hall of Mirrors place?" Luke asked, so I described it.

He said, "Oh. I thought you meant like a House of Mirrors at a fairground."

It was my turn to look puzzled. Naturally, I'd never been to a fairground.

Luke explained, "It's like a sort of maze where some of the walls are glass and some are mirrors. You pay to go in and try to find your way out. You walk into what you think is an opening, but it's glass. You see somebody coming towards you – it's your own reflection. And some of the mirrors make you look weird."

"And people pay money for that?" I said. "Now that is weird, if you ask me."

39

"Yeah, it's really stupid, when they could go on the scary rides instead," said Dylan.

"People pay to get scared? I don't understand that either."

"You would, if you tried it," said Luke. "Haven't you ever been on a roller-coaster or a dark ride?"

"No."

Dylan said, "Rebecca's led a sheltered life – I told you. Her family doesn't have anything to do with modern things. No TV, no computer, no mobile phone – nothing."

"How do you know that?" I asked him, because I'd never discussed it with him.

"When I told my foster mum about you, she knew a bit about the group you belong to. There are lots of strict rules, right? And you're not supposed to mix with anybody from outside."

"I shouldn't really be talking to you now," I said. "I wouldn't be, if Lois was here."

"But that's terrible," said Luke. "It's like... it's like a prison, or something."

"No it isn't. They get to watch TV in prison," Dylan said.

Luke asked, "Why do you put up with it? Why don't you leave?"

"It would be sinful to leave. God would be angry – that's what my dad says. And if we did leave, nobody would ever speak to us again."

"You should come to our church," said Luke. "You'd find out that you can follow God without keeping all those rules."

"I wouldn't be allowed to. The Chosen Prophet – that's our leader – says the churches have been infected by the sins of the world. We have to keep away from them."

Luke and Dylan exchanged glances. It was a look that meant, *She's crazy, but she can't help it. You have to feel sorry for her.*

I hated that – I wanted to get back to when Dylan and I were just talking to each other like friends.

"None of this is getting us any closer to the lost money," I said. "I could ask my mum if you can come to the Hall again. Maybe you could both come."

"That would be great," said Luke.

Dylan said, "Why do you want to look for the treasure, Rebecca? Money is the root of all evil, isn't it?"

"The *love* of money is the root of all evil," I corrected him. "And I don't really want the money. I'm interested, that's all. I lead a pretty boring life. As you know."

They laughed. Luke said, "Well, I'll have your share if you don't want it. My sister has got to go to America soon, and we don't have the money for the air fares. Mum's going to have to try and borrow it."

He looked worried. Like Dylan's ghost search, this was a serious matter for him.

41

"I'll help you if I can," I said. "I'll ask Mum tonight, and call you if she says yes. Here – write down your phone number."

"What? You're allowed to use a phone?" Dylan pretended to be shocked.

"An ordinary phone, yes. It's mobile phones that aren't allowed."

As I said it, I realised how crazy this sounded. Because I was used to keeping the rule, I had never seen how odd it was. I would have to ask Dad about it – there was sure to be a reason, although it was rather hard to find any mention of phones in the Bible.

The boys both wrote down their home phone numbers, and I hid them away in the depths of my pencil case.

"I'll call you tonight," I promised.

Chapter 7:

Reflections

"Dad never said Dylan wasn't allowed back to the Hall," I reminded Mum. "He only said not to let him into our house."

"Well..." Mum said, and I could tell she was wavering.

"And anyway, Dad isn't going to be here."

Dad had gone to Manchester for some special Meetings. The Leader, the Chosen Prophet, would be speaking. It was a great honour to be invited – only a few of the men from our group were going, and none of the women. So Dad would never find out about Dylan coming back.

In the end Mum said Dylan and Luke could both come to the Hall. They came on Saturday morning, just as the painters arrived to work on the Yellow Room. Because she was busy with the painters, Mum let me take charge of the boys.

"She must have decided that you won't try to steal the silver teaspoons," I said.

Luke said, "Just suppose we did find the Earl's missing money. Who would it belong to? Could we keep it?"

None of us knew the answer to this.

"We would get a reward for finding it, I'm sure," I said.

43

"It might not be money that we should be looking for," said Dylan. "The old Earl might have spent it on something else, like gold bars or diamonds."

"Or chocolate buttons, or teddy bears," I said. "Don't forget, he ended up in a madhouse."

"So, we don't know what we're looking for, we don't know where it is, we don't know if we can keep it if we find it... or if it even exists." Dylan seemed to be losing enthusiasm for treasure-hunting. Perhaps he would prefer to go looking for ghosts.

But when we came into the Hall of Mirrors, he got interested again. We all did. We opened the mirrored doors into the bedrooms, trying to see if there could be a concealed room or a secret passage. But all we found was a hidden cupboard full of mops and brooms, which I already knew about.

I caught a glimpse of my own reflection every now and then. Each time, I looked away quickly. What would Dylan and Luke think of my odd, old-fashioned clothes? I would have worn my school things, even though it was Saturday, because they looked more normal than my weekend clothes. But Mum had already put my school clothes in the wash.

Then I told myself not to be so silly. They were boys. They probably didn't care about my clothes, or even notice them. The only thing on their minds was the treasure.

Dylan was going slowly down the long room, touching and pressing things. But none of the marble panels moved under his hand. The gold-painted carvings stayed firmly in place.

Luke examined the floor with its zigzag pattern of polished wood. It was old, and there were small gaps between some of the sections. One or two pieces were actually loose, but all that lay beneath was more wood.

Walls, floor... that left the ceiling. I gazed up at it. High and curved, it was covered with faded paintings. Enormous glass chandeliers hung down from it like stalactites in a cave. There was no way of reaching it without a ladder.

Then I had a thought. This ceiling... wasn't it a bit higher than the bedroom ceilings? I went to check.

The ceilings in the bedrooms, although high compared to a modern house, were definitely lower than in the Hall of Mirrors. When I told the boys, they saw the importance of this at once.

"There could be an empty space up there. A kind of attic," said Luke.

"No, the actual attic is even higher up," I said. "But there could be an empty space above the bedroom ceilings."

If there was, we couldn't find any way of getting to it. The bedroom ceilings had no panels or doors in them as far as we could see.

"Maybe you can get to it from above," Dylan said.

We hurried upstairs into the servants' area. There was no opening in the floor of the long corridor. But possibly, in one of those locked rooms...

I went to ask Mum to unlock the doors for us. As we came up the stairs, she asked me what we were doing. When I told her, she laughed.

"You're right, there is a space under the top floor. I know I've seen a trapdoor in one of the rooms. But I don't think you'll find any hidden treasure."

"Can't we at least look?"

"All right. No climbing about inside, though. I don't want anyone falling through the ceiling."

In the top corridor, the boys were waiting outside one particular door. As Mum unlocked it, Dylan whispered, "We think this is the room in the photo. We counted the doors."

So this was the room where that "ghostly face" had been captured on camera! I looked around. There was a bit more furniture than in the previous rooms we'd seen – a table, two iron bedsteads, a cracked mirror...

"No trapdoor," I said, disappointed.

"Yes there is," Luke said, excited. "Under the bed – see."

We dragged the heavy bed to one side, raising a cloud of dust. Now I could see a square shape cut into the floorboards, a sort of hinged panel with a metal ring as a handle.

Luke grasped the handle and pulled. The trapdoor lifted. Below lay a dark, shadowy space. Wooden beams ran across it, holding up the ceiling of the room below. As far as we could see, the space was empty.

I had brought a torch with me in case we needed it. I leaned through the door, shining the light around. On one side the roof of the Hall of Mirrors curved over like the body of a whale. A long pipe snaked away into the darkness. Everything was covered with the dust of 250 years.

"There's nothing valuable in there," I said, getting up.

"Are you sure?" said Luke. "Let me try."

I gave him the torch. Meanwhile, Dylan had gone over to the window. I guessed he was thinking about the girl who had killed herself – perhaps by jumping from this very window. And about the pale shape in the photograph, which might be her ghost.

Suddenly I noticed something.

"Dylan," I said, "I think I've seen the ghost."

"What?" He spun round.

"I mean, I've found out what looked like a ghost in that picture. It was that mirror... look!"

The small oval mirror was hanging on a nail in the side of the window recess, where the light was at its brightest in the dingy room. Long ago, a servant probably used it to comb her hair and make sure her cap was pinned on straight.

"The mirror is in exactly the spot where that pale shape appeared in the photo," I said. "At the side, about half way up. On a bright day, if the sun's at the right angle, it probably shows up in photos. And it's just the right shape for a face."

Dylan stared at it. I could tell he didn't want me to be right, and yet he could see the logic of what I was saying. He looked so let down, I almost wished I'd kept my mouth shut. This was turning out to be a disappointing morning.

All at once, Luke shouted, "I've found something! Look at this!"

Chapter 8:
Rules

Luke was holding a tiny box in the palm of his hand. It was covered in velvet, faded to a dark grey, and the hinges were golden.

"It was in that pile of rubbish," he said, pointing down. I saw the marks of his fingers in the dust and broken plaster that lay below the trapdoor.

"Open it, then," said Dylan.

"Can I?" Luke asked my mum, and she nodded.

He opened the little box carefully. Inside was a plain gold ring, gleaming dully, and a piece of yellowed paper, tightly folded up.

"That looks like a wedding ring," said Mum. "Why would it be hidden away like that?"

"Maybe the paper will tell us," I said.

Very carefully, because the paper was old and had been folded so tightly, Mum opened it up. "It's a marriage certificate," she said, peering at the ornate, curling handwriting. "*County of Dumfries, 1914, on the twentieth day of December...*"

"Who got married, Mum?" I asked impatiently.

"Frank Albert Jacob, Viscount Mallenford, Second Lt in the Denshire Rifles. He married Laura... no, Lorna... Marshall, housemaid. He was 22, she was 16."

"So it really happened!" I said. "It's like something in a book. The Earl's son fell in love with the housemaid.

49

And they got married secretly – it must have been secret, or else why did she hide the ring?"

"The Earl wouldn't have approved," said Mum.

"What about Lorna's family – what did they think? She was only 16, after all."

Mum read some more of the slanting handwriting. "Her parents were dead. John Marshall, coachman, and Annie Margaret Marshall, both deceased. She was an orphan, poor girl."

"1914," said Dylan thoughtfully. "The war had started. Frank must have known he would soon be sent to fight in France."

"So they got married in secret and had a few days of happiness," I said, "and then he went away. Lorna went back to being a housemaid. Like Cinderella after the ball, dreaming that her prince would come and find her."

But that never happened. A few weeks or months later, she heard the dreaded news that Frank had been killed. The dream turned into a nightmare. She'd lost the man she loved. Perhaps she was expecting a baby. What was she going to do?

I remembered the story Mrs Dawkins had told. Inside the locked room, Lorna had cried, "It's gone! They've taken it!" She must have meant the ring and the marriage certificate. In her panic she couldn't find them, and she thought they had been stolen.

The man she loved was dead. Without proof of the marriage, nobody would believe she was his wife. If she had a child, everyone would call her a slut. They would throw her out, along with her baby. She had nothing left to live for… so she jumped to her death.

"That's terrible," said Dylan.

"It wouldn't happen nowadays," Luke said. "People don't care if girls have babies without getting married."

Mum gave him a disapproving look. She was going to think he was a bad influence, talking like that. She might stop me seeing Dylan and Luke – and I really didn't want that. They had started to seem almost like friends.

"What will happen to the ring?" I said, changing the subject.

"I'll have to write to Miss Morton about it," said Mum. "I suppose it officially belongs to her, since she owns the house."

"So we can't keep it?" asked Dylan.

"Of course not."

"Don't you think she might give Luke a reward for finding it?" I said.

"We'll just have to wait and see," said Mum.

★ ★ ★

Dad came home on Sunday night. He said the meetings had been very good. The Chosen Prophet, our leader, had spoken three times, and he had some important new instructions for every member of the Meeting.

51

"The Day of the Lord, the Day of Judgement, is near, and we have to be ready. We must get rid of all worldly influences. We mustn't own any books, except for Bible study and school books. Women are not to work outside their homes..."

He went on with a long list, but I'd stopped listening. No books! I couldn't believe it! Books were my lifeline. Books stopped me from dying of boredom. And they were my only way of learning about life outside the narrow walls of the Meeting.

I once read a poem about a lady who was imprisoned in a tower under an evil spell. If she ever looked out of the window, she would die. So she used a mirror to look at the world outside. Books were my mirror – and now they were being taken away. *The mirror crack'd from side to side...*

"Dad, you're not serious, are you?" I said. "About books being banned?"

"Books are not banned," he said. "The Chosen Prophet says we should read the Bible, of course, and books about Christian living, and school books for study."

"But stories... fiction... can't we read that kind of book any more?"

"No."

When he saw the look of horror on my face, he softened a little. "At least, we mustn't have them in the house. That's what the Chosen Prophet said. He didn't mention reading them in school, so perhaps..."

"If I do, Lois will see," I said. "And she'll tell her father."

Mum had a different problem. "Did you say that women are not to work outside the home?"

"That's right. The Chosen Prophet says that a woman's most vital work is caring for her husband and children. She can't put them first if she has a paid job to do."

"But James! If I have to give up work, we won't have enough to live on. We couldn't afford to run the car. We might even have to move – this house goes with the job, remember?"

"God will provide, if we are obedient," Dad said. *"Seek ye first the kingdom of God, and his righteousness, and all these things shall be added unto you."*

He looked, as usual, strong and determined, certain that he was right. Mum and I exchanged glances. I saw that Mum was as shocked by these new rules as I was.

But what could we do? There were only two choices: obey the rules or leave the Meeting. And if we left, Dad would never be allowed to see us again. Nor would my cousins, or anyone we knew. We would be left alone in a world full of sinful strangers, like lost sheep wandering on a cold, lonely mountain.

"When do these new rules come in?" Mum asked.

"Straight away," he said. "Rebecca, I want you to get all your books together, ready to be burned."

"Burned!" I cried. "Can't I just give them to a charity shop?"

"But my job," said Mum, looking dazed. "I have to give at least a month's notice."

"That's all right. The Chosen Prophet understands that these things can't be arranged in a hurry. He's allowing three months, but after that, married women are not to do paid work any more."

That night, I lay in bed seething with rage. I couldn't bear to think of a life without books. I hated the thought of the books that I loved going up in smoke.

I could try to hide them, or some of them. But our house was so small, there was no hiding place for anything bigger than a matchbox.

What about the Hall, though? There was a big room full of books there. Mum called it the Library, although the books were not for lending out. Most of them looked heavy and old-fashioned, not the sort of thing anyone would want to read. I could hide my books there quite safely.

I would have to get Mum on my side, though. Without the alarm code, I couldn't get into the Hall.

Then I had an even better idea. The Folly! In that fake ruin, there were a couple of rooms with proper roofs over them. If I wrapped my books in a bin-liner to keep them dry, I could hide them there, and read them whenever I wanted to. No one ever went into the Folly.

The thought crossed my mind that I was disobeying the Chosen Prophet. Perhaps I was disobeying God himself. But I didn't care. I was sick to death of all those stupid rules.

Chapter 9:
History lesson

There were just a few days of school left before the start of the summer holiday. I was dreading it. Unlike lots of other people in my class, I wouldn't be going away on holiday – that was another rule of the Meeting. I would be stuck at home all summer, bored and lonely.

Lois was back in school, so I couldn't talk easily to Dylan or Luke. This was annoying, for I had some news. Mum had written to Miss Morton about the wedding ring. Miss Morton rang as soon as she got the letter. She wanted Mum to show the ring to a local historian who was writing a book about the Mallenford family.

When Mum put the phone down, I said, "You didn't tell Miss Morton you'll be leaving your job."

"I'm hoping I won't have to," Mum said. "I still have three months, and maybe the Chosen Prophet will change his mind about what he said. He's done that before."

"Has he?" I said, surprised. I'd always been told that the Leader's words came straight from God.

"Yes, he has. A few times. But people seem to have forgotten that."

"Mum, do you think the things he says are really... well, really from God?"

Mum hesitated. Then she said, "I used to think so. But now I'm not so sure. Some of his rules aren't in line with the Bible, and that can't be right."

"Why does everybody else in the Meeting believe every word he says?" I cried. "Why don't they ever think he might be wrong?"

"Shhh. Your dad's coming in. We'll talk about this later."

★ ★ ★

The historian arrived on Thursday evening. She turned out to be a woman. Her name was Hannah Conway; she looked about Mum's age, with dark curly hair and a nice smile. I had already asked Mum if I could be there when she looked at the ring.

We sat at the polished table in the Blue Room. Mum pulled up the blinds to give more light. Specks of dust swirled around in the evening sunlight, and Mum sighed. "You never get finished with dusting this place," she said.

Hannah asked me how we had found the ring, and I told her all about it. Then she took a careful look at the marriage certificate.

"This is very interesting," she said. "It ties in with something that Frank's father, the seventh Earl, wrote in a letter to a friend of his. He was upset because Frank had been posted abroad, but had chosen not to spend

Christmas at home with his family. Frank told his father he was visiting an old school friend."

"But really he was getting married," I said.

"So it would seem. Then he was sent to fight in the trenches, and a few months later – in April 1915 – he was shot at Ypres. He never saw his father again."

"Or his wife," I said.

"Have you read any more letters from the Earl?" Mum asked.

"Oh, yes. There's quite a collection of them in the museum at Lowfield."

"Were any of them written after he disappeared?" I asked eagerly.

Hannah shook her head. "That part of his life is a complete mystery. We have letters written all through the war, but nothing after February 1919. In the later ones, he sounds totally grief-stricken. He can't get over the loss of his three sons."

"Poor man," said Mum.

"He wasn't poor at all. He was loaded with money," I said.

"Money couldn't buy him happiness," said Mum. "*Do not trust in the uncertainty of riches, but in God.*"

Hannah gave her an odd kind of look. Perhaps she didn't realise that Mum was quoting from the Bible.

I said, "What sort of things did the Earl write about in his letters?"

"Well, after his sons were killed, he became quite obsessed with the fact that the Mallenford line was dying out. He was in his sixties, a bit too old to remarry and start another family. But then he met one of Frank's comrades – a soldier who had fought beside him in France four years earlier. And this man told him that Frank had mentioned a wife, but the soldier couldn't remember her name or anything about her. The Earl wrote that he was going to try and find this wife, if she existed."

"She was already dead," I said, and I told Hannah what we knew of Lorna. "It was hopeless looking for her. No wonder he went crazy."

Mum said, "How would he have tried to find out about her?"

"Well, he could have enquired at Somerset House, which held the records of all marriages in England and Wales. But I see this marriage took place in Scotland. I don't know if he would have thought of going there."

Mum asked Hannah if she wanted to see the place where the ring had lain hidden for so long. Hannah said she would like to see the entire house, so we gave her a tour. Mum was being quite chatty, which was unusual. She showed Hannah everything, even the kitchens and the cellars that visitors didn't get to see.

"Is it interesting, being a historian?" I asked her, as we came back towards the entrance.

"Yes, very. At least I think so! What do you want to be when you grow up?"

"I suppose I'll get married and have kids," I muttered.

"But don't you want to study? You're obviously a bright girl. You could go to university."

I said nothing. Girls from the Meeting didn't go to university. It just didn't happen.

Hannah turned to look at me. Her glance took in my clothes and my headscarf.

"You know, when I was your age, I wore clothes rather like yours," she said. "My family belonged to a Sunday Meeting group in London."

This took me completely by surprise. She didn't look anything like a member of the Meeting.

"Really?" I said. "What happened?"

Hannah said, "We were put out of the Meeting when I was 14. My dad had an argument with the Elders, and they cut us off completely. It was very difficult at first. We'd been taught that there were no true Christians outside the Meeting. But we found that was a lie. There are lots of people who believe in God and follow him. And some of them helped us."

Mum said, "But most people who call themselves Christians don't live holy lives. They don't read God's word and obey it like we do. God must hate them."

"Do you think that if you obey God, you can force him to love you?" said Hannah. "The Bible says, *There is no one righteous – not even one.* However hard people try, they can never be good enough. They make the rules stricter, they watch one another more closely, and yet they never really know God's love."

I wanted to say: that's exactly how I feel! I don't know if God loves me. I never feel good enough.

"But God does love us," Hannah went on. "If we stop trying to make ourselves perfect... if we tell him we're sorry for our mistakes, and ask him to forgive us... he will do it, every time. He'll wash away all the wrong we've done. He'll make us clean again, perfect. Whiter than snow."

On Mum's face I could see a look of longing. Like me, she wanted to hear more of this.

Then her lips tightened. It was as if she'd suddenly remembered who she was talking to... an outsider, an unbeliever, wearing make-up and worldly clothes.

"I know what you're saying. It's in the Bible – Psalm 51," she said. "And now, if you don't mind, time's getting on. I really should be locking the place up."

Hannah said, "Of course. I'm very grateful to you for showing me around. Could I come back another time? I would like to take some photos for the book that I'm writing."

"All right," said Mum.

"Here's my phone number. If ever you want to get in touch with me for any reason, just call me. Any reason. I mean that."

She wrote her number on a piece of paper, and Mum took it. But as Hannah drove away, Mum crumpled up the paper and dropped it on the ground.

Chapter 10:

The last day

The last day of school would be my only chance to see Dylan until next term. He wanted to see me, too. He had some news, he said.

"Try to get away from that friend of yours, and meet us round the back of the Physics lab," he said.

"What friend? She's not my friend."

By going in at one entrance to the toilets and coming out at the other, I managed to shake Lois off. She would be annoyed, but I couldn't help that.

I told Dylan and Luke about Hannah's visit. "And she took the ring away to get it looked at by an expert. She said it was historically interesting. But she didn't think it would be worth much in actual money."

"So, no reward then," Luke said, disappointed. "We really need some money. My mum can't borrow any more on her credit card."

"You said you had some news," I reminded Dylan.

"Oh, yes. Look what we found on the internet. I was doing a search on "Mallenford Hall", and this came up. It's the diary of an Aussie who fought in World War One. His grandson, or somebody, put it on a website."

Dylan explained that the Australian soldier had been wounded by shrapnel. He had spent several weeks at the Hall, which had been turned into a military hospital. Then he was sent back to the battlefield.

"There's a lot of stuff about the fighting and how horrible it was," said Luke. "But that's not the interesting bit."

Dylan said, "When the war was over, he was heading for Liverpool to get on a ship back to Australia. On the way, he stopped off at Mallenford. He wanted to go back to the Hall and see this nurse that he used to like.

"He found that the gates were locked. The Hall wasn't a hospital any more. In fact it looked empty, with no lights on. But he needed somewhere to sleep that night, so he climbed over the gate. Here – read it. Read what he wrote."

Saw a light, not at the main building, but up the hill at the ruined castle. There was an old beggar dossing down inside – crazy-looking chap with a grey beard. He had a fire going, quite cosy. Gave me some soup, said that any soldier was a friend of his. Asked me if I'd seen his sons, fighting on the Western Front. Then he looked kind of confused and said, no, I wouldn't have seen them because they were dead.

"It was the Earl!" I said.

"Yes. That's what we think."

"But why was he living in the Folly? The Hall still belonged to him, didn't it?"

"He was crazy," said Dylan.

I said, "Maybe he couldn't bear to live there. It would keep on reminding him of his family."

"Or maybe he was living at the Folly because that's where his treasure was. He dug a hole and buried it," said Luke.

"We have to have a proper look," said Dylan. "Can you get us into the grounds, Rebecca?"

"I might be able to. It would have to be when Dad and Mum aren't around," I said. "I'll ring you. Don't call me in case my dad answers the phone."

As we went back into school, bad luck came to meet us – Lois was coming out. She saw the three of us, and her eyes gleamed.

"You've been talking to those boys again," she said in a shocked voice. "What will your dad say?"

"My dad's not going to know unless you tell people, Lois. And I'll know that it was you who did it. And I'll never speak to you again."

"Oh, don't be horrible. Why can't we be friends?"

"We are friends," I forced myself to say, "as long as you don't get me into trouble."

"Good." She linked arms with me. "Can I come and visit you during the holidays? I'd love to see where you live."

We went past some girls from my class.

"Oh look, it's the Scarf Sisters," I heard one of them say. "They're like Siamese twins, never separated." And the others giggled. I felt my face burn with embarrassment.

Someone else said. "They think they're better than everybody else. Stuck-up cows!"

64

Lois swung round. "We *are* better than you. We keep God's laws and you don't."

The girls stared at her as if she was something not quite human – an alien from a distant planet.

"Oh yeah? Does God say you have to dress like an old bag lady? If so, I'm glad I don't believe in him."

"Me too."

Lois said, "You'll change your minds on the Last Day – the Day of Judgement. But then it will be too late."

She had a smug look on her face as we walked down the corridor. "I'm glad I got the chance to witness to those girls. I don't think they'll forget what I said."

No, Lois. They won't.

Suddenly I felt glad that it was the last day of term. Really, Lois was nothing but trouble. I didn't want to go around with her, and I certainly didn't want people calling me her twin.

The faces of those girls, like a row of mirrors, had shown me what our image was like to people outside the Meeting. To them, Lois and I seemed like freaks – totally weird. Lois didn't seem to care about that, but I did.

I just wanted to be ordinary, normal. I wanted to have friends and be like the other girls. But I was trapped inside the uniform and the rules of the Meeting.

Would I have to spend the rest of my life like this? I didn't think I could bear it.

★ ★ ★

Next day, Mum and Dad were going shopping, but I said I would rather stay at home. As soon as they'd left, I tried calling Dylan's house, but no one answered. At Luke's house, his mum said he had gone out on his bike. I felt annoyed. This was a wasted opportunity.

But perhaps I could find some more clues, all by myself. Dylan and Luke would be really impressed if I did.

Ever since I was 9 or 10, I had been allowed to roam around the grounds of the Hall on my own. It was quite safe, Dad said. No strangers could get in; there was a high wall around the outside, and the gates were kept locked. So I went out, heading for the Folly.

It looked quite large from a distance, with its tower and battlements. When you got closer, you saw that the tower wasn't much higher than a two-storey house. The doorway and the window slits were small, to make the building seem bigger.

The walls, which looked ruined, in fact were solidly built. Inside were two little rooms, with stone roofs and floors, but no glass in the windows. They didn't look too comfortable to live in. It was all very primitive compared to the Hall.

If the Earl had really been living here, he must have been rather lonely, I thought. Even crazy people could feel lonely. Or had loneliness driven him crazy?

I checked that my bag of books was still safe, buried in a pile of dry leaves that had collected in a corner. Then I climbed the spiral steps to the flat roof of the tower. From up here, you could look down towards the Hall. In the opposite direction, the woods stretched out into the distance, seemingly without a break. The boundary wall was somewhere out there, hidden in the trees.

If you had money that you wanted to keep safe, where would you put it? Perhaps the Folly had a secret room. Or you could easily dig a hole somewhere in the depths of the wood – the problem would be finding it again.

There was quite a lot of writing carved, or scratched unevenly, on the battlements of the tower. People had left their initials there, with the date they had visited the place. Most of the dates were during the First World War, during the time when the Hall was a hospital. Graffiti, it seemed, had been around for a long time before spray-cans were invented.

Suddenly I thought I heard a sound – someone moving about downstairs. But there shouldn't be anyone here! Mum and Dad couldn't possibly be back yet. They would have locked the gates when they left.

I started to feel quite scared. I was all alone, except for... who?

Just keep quiet, I told myself, and maybe whoever it is will go away. Stay still. Don't move.

But then I heard the sound of feet coming up the stairs. Closer and closer they came. And there was nowhere to hide – nowhere at all.

Chapter 11:
The folly and the fountain

At the top of the stairs, a head came into view. I laughed aloud – for the "stranger" was Luke. He jumped at the sound of my voice.

"Rebecca! What are you doing here?"

"Same as you, I expect. Is Dylan with you?"

"No. He's gone out for the day."

"How did you get in? Did my dad forget to lock the gate?"

He shook his head. "I went around the outside of the wall. I followed it into the woods, and I found a place where it's broken down."

I remembered Dad had mentioned that a fallen tree had damaged the wall. He said he would rebuild it in the winter, when there wasn't much gardening work to do. He had thought that nobody would see the broken section because it was deep in the woods. But Luke had discovered it. I was impressed... Luke was really determined to find the treasure.

At the same time I felt a bit annoyed. What right did he have to come in here? This was *my* place, *my* garden. He should have waited for me to call him and invite him in.

But he couldn't wait – I soon saw that when he explained about his sister. She was only eight and she had cancer. A few months earlier, she had gone to America to try out a new treatment, which had helped her. She was supposed to go back for a check-up quite soon. The air fares for his sister and his mum would cost hundreds of pounds.

"And we just don't have the money," he said. "Mum already had to borrow a lot of money for the last trip. My dad would help, but he's always skint. I got myself a paper round, but that doesn't earn much. So I'm going to keep looking for the Mallenford millions."

"Let's get started, then," I said.

The walls of the Folly were built of rough stone, like the castle it was meant to be. There were small gaps between many of the stones where the mortar had crumbled away. We worked our way slowly around the building, poking sticks into the gaps, looking for... what exactly? That was part of the trouble. We didn't know.

Luke kicked aside the leaves on the floor, finding my bag of books at once. He only glanced at it, though.

"This is nothing to do with the treasure," he said. "These books are much newer than that. Are they yours?"

"Yes."

"Why have you hidden them here?"

I explained about the latest set of rules. He said, "That's totally crazy. I don't understand why you have to obey all these rules."

"Because God has told us to."

"How? I'm pretty sure the Bible doesn't say anything about not reading books."

"God speaks to our leader, the Chosen Prophet, and tells him what we are to do," I said. "Sometimes I think the Chosen Prophet could be getting it wrong. But everybody else is so sure he's right."

Luke said, "Listen, I believe in God too, but he's not like your God. Your God sounds like... I don't know... like a strict teacher, watching out for people's mistakes."

"It says in the Bible that he watches us."

"Yes, but not like a teacher. More like a good father watching over his child."

I said nothing. My own father often felt like a strict teacher, keeping an eye on me. I knew he loved me, and yet I was sometimes afraid of him. It was the same with God.

Luke said, "I don't think people can ever find their way to God by keeping rules."

"How do you think we can know God, then?"

He hesitated, looking for the right words. "If we tell him we're sorry for the wrong things we've done, he forgives us. If we open the door of our lives, he comes in. And then he... sort of lives inside us. It's hard to explain..."

As he spoke, he was looking out of the window in the direction of the Hall. He said, "That big house, it's all clean and tidy and well-kept. But nobody actually lives there."

I thought it was odd of him to change the subject so suddenly. But he went on, "Those rules and regulations are like that. People's lives are clean and tidy-looking, but if God doesn't live inside them, they're empty."

Empty… yes, that was how I often felt. But I wasn't ready to admit it. I couldn't believe that Luke, an ordinary boy who broke all the rules of the Meeting, might know God better than I did.

"Come on," I said, "we're wasting time. My mum and dad will be back soon."

As we went on with our search, I thought about what he had said. And I wondered why it was so easy to talk to Dylan and Luke. I couldn't have had this conversation with any of the girls at school, not even with Lois.

Was it easier because they were boys? The girls at school only seemed interested in clothes and parties and boyfriends and TV. That was what they mostly talked about. Luke and Dylan were interested in different things – things that I could share in without feeling left out.

Maybe when groups of boys got together, they only talked about football. I wouldn't know. But I was glad I had got to know Luke and Dylan. I was determined not to break up this new friendship… even if Dad didn't approve.

★ ★ ★

After a while, we decided that the Folly was a waste of time. The building was too empty to give good hiding places. But what about the woods?

Apart from the grassy pathway which Dad mowed now and then, there were woods all around the Folly. Bramble bushes and rhododendrons made a jungle at ground level. Little animal tracks wandered about, leading nowhere in particular.

"It wouldn't have been overgrown like this in the old days," I said. "There were gardeners to keep it tidy. Dad says it would have looked more like a park than a wood."

"But after the War, when the old Earl was camping out here – what would it have looked like then?" asked Luke. "Maybe it would already have started to go wild."

I remembered a line from a detective story. "Where does a wise man hide a leaf? In the forest."

"Concentrate, girl. It's not leaves we're looking for."

"What *are* we looking for? A place where something was buried nearly 100 years ago? It will all be overgrown by now. There won't be anything to see."

He refused to be put off. He said, "You take the north side, I'll take the south."

"Okay, but make sure you stay hidden in the trees. If my dad sees you, he'll go mad."

I wandered along a badger trail, avoiding the thorny brambles which kept trying to snare my skirt. I was thinking the task was hopeless, when suddenly I heard a shout. "Come and see this!"

"What is it? What have you found?"

"I don't know. A sort of stone thing. Come and look."

"Oh, that," I said, when I saw what he was looking at. "It's always been there. I think it must have been a fountain in the old days."

It was a white marble bowl about four feet wide, with a small statue to one side. The bowl was empty and half-covered in ivy. The statue was old, its edges blurred by time. Maybe it was meant to be a girl or an angel – you couldn't really tell. It held a marble vase with a piece of rusting pipe sticking out. There wasn't even a trickle of water.

Luke was excited to have found something. He didn't care about my lack of interest. He started pulling strands of ivy away from the carved stone.

The plants were not deep-rooted. They came away easily. Looking down, I saw a narrow, slit-like gap between the earth and the marble base of the statue. Sliding my fingers down the side of the stone, I touched something that wasn't stone and wasn't earth.

"There's something down there!"

We scrabbled the earth away with our hands. Eagerly, I picked up the thing that had been slipped down the side of the statue.

It was a black metal box, not much bigger than a pencil case. The edges were brown with rust. There was a keyhole, but no key. When I shook it, it rattled slightly, as if something small was moving about inside.

"I'll smash it open with a stone," said Luke.

"No, don't do that. We don't know what's inside – you could damage it."

We stared at the mysterious box. It gave nothing away. There was no name or initial on it. It didn't feel heavy. Certainly there couldn't be a vast sum of money inside.

"It might be nothing to do with the treasure," I said. "It could be anything."

"Like what?"

"A servant's life savings. Letters to a wounded soldier. Anything."

"You don't really think that," said Luke.

"No."

"We have got to open it," he said. "And I know somebody who could help us. Vince – that's Dylan's foster dad – is a carpenter. He's got all kinds of tools."

"Take it to him, then," I said. "Go on. What are you waiting for?"

Chapter 12:

Letters

Two days went by. I was longing to know if they had managed to open the box, but I couldn't ring Luke or Dylan until Monday, when Mum and Dad had both gone to work. Finally I got through to Dylan's house.

"Well? What did you find?"

"Nothing valuable. Not even a map with *X marks the spot*," he said, sounding disappointed. "Only a key – we don't know what for – and a couple of letters. Do you want to see them?"

"Of course I want to see them!"

We arranged to meet at the fountain that afternoon. It would be safer than the Folly, where Dad might happen to look up from his work and see us going in.

The boys were late. I waited impatiently, unable to sit down. By the time they arrived, my pacing feet had worn a path through the undergrowth.

At last they reached me, and Dylan opened his backpack. The letters, old and yellowing, were inside a plastic folder. "The tin was so rusty, it fell apart when Vince tried to open it," he explained.

There was a key too – a small, old-fashioned looking key in dark grey metal. I turned it around in my hand, wondering if it fitted a lock somewhere in the Hall. There were dozens of keyholes in doors, wardrobes, cabinets and cupboards. The only way to find out would be to try.

Then I opened out the first letter. It was hand-written in that old-fashioned writing. There was no address at the top, only a date, 27th February 1919.

Dear Lord Mallenford,

Please excuse me for writing to you. It is something I never wanted to do, but needs must. In December of 1914, I got married to your son Frank at Hopetoun. We ran away together because we knew you would not approve, me being only a servant girl. But we loved each other dearly and it was a great sorrow to me when Frank never returned from the wars.

The only light in my darkness is my son, who is now 4 years old and the image of his poor father. I have tried to bring him up as dear Frank would have wished, but we are very poor and it is difficult. If only you could send me a small amount of money now and then, I would promise never to trouble you. The money would all be used for little Frankie. You could send it to me at the Post Office at George Street in Edinburgh.

With humble gratitude,

Iona Mallenford (Mrs)

"That's weird," I said. "Who's this Iona person? Did the Earl's son get married twice?"

"Not unless he did it in the same month at the same place to two different women," said Dylan. "Think about it, Rebecca."

Luke said, "Think about those names. Iona... Lorna.... Imagine them written in that curly writing."

"Yes. If you didn't already know Lorna's name, you could easily misread it," I said.

Dylan said, "What we think is, this other woman found out about the marriage somehow, maybe from the marriage records at Hopetoun. But she got the name wrong."

"She read the word *housemaid* all right, though," said Luke. "And she guessed it was a runaway marriage, or why would they have gone all the way to Scotland, where the laws were different?"

"Wait a minute," I said. "How could she know that Frank was dead?"

"Vince says she could have looked it up. There would have been a notice of his death in the *Times*. Or in the big book where all the lords and dukes and people are listed."

"So what was she trying to do?"

"To get money, of course," said Dylan. "The Earl might send her some money for his non-existent grandchild. Or he might pay her to keep it secret that his son had run off with a servant."

"What a horrible woman," I said. "I wonder if he paid her anything."

"Read the next letter," said Luke.

This one was typed, much easier to read. It was from the Strand Private Detective Agency in London, addressed not to the Earl of Mallenford but to a Mr Smith in Fitzroy Square, Mayfair. ("But it could have been the Earl giving a false name," said Dylan.)

May 2nd, 1919

Dear Mr Smith,

We have investigated the marriage records at Hopetoun in Dumfriesshire. It certainly appears that a marriage took place on the 20th December 1914, between Frank, Viscount Mallenford and a Laura, or possibly Lorna, Mitchell or Marshall, who gave her address as 1 Church Street, Denfield. (This address, by the way, is fictitious. There is no such street in Denfield.)

We then made inquiries at the Post Office in George Street, Edinburgh. It is a busy post office, with many customers. However, two of the clerks recalled a woman who used to come in quite often, asking if there were any letters for her. She appeared middle-aged and was always dressed in black. She was notable for the fact that she asked for letters addressed to several different names: not only Mallenford, but Maclean, Dale, Huntingdon, and others which they could not remember.

For weeks she had been a frequent visitor, collecting several items of mail. Then she stopped coming in. The post office clerks asked me if the police had arrested her. They believed she was involved in some kind of criminal activity, and I must say that it seems likely. The woman calling herself Iona Mallenford is probably an impostor. She may already be in the hands of the police, or she may have fled, fearing an arrest.

If we can be of any further service to you, please let us know. I enclose our bill to the sum of £27 11/6d.

Yours sincerely,

J. Frobisher.

"It sounds like something out of Sherlock Holmes," I said.

"Sherlock Holmes would have found out a lot more information than that lot did," Luke said gloomily.

"Yes, he'd probably have found out that Lorna Marshall was already dead," said Dylan. "And that would have stopped the Earl doing what he did next. Keep on reading, Rebecca."

There was one more letter. The handwriting was very hard to read, and in places the ink seemed to have dissolved, as if damp had seeped into the paper.

My dear Charles,

I am about to set out on a quest. Do you remember the quests of our boyhood – hunting dragons and rescuing fair ladies? I hope you also remember our secret hiding place by the fountain, where I will place this letter before I set out. I would like to leave some record of what I am about to do; I am aware that my memory is failing badly. Today is a good day. Sometimes I can hardly remember my own name!

You will see from the enclosed letter that my son Frank made a secret marriage shortly before he was sent to France. He never discussed this, as far as I am aware, with any member of the family. He probably knew we would try to dissuade him; it was a most unsuitable marriage.

However, I cannot help wondering if there was a child of the marriage. If so, he would be the last heir to the Mallenford name and fortune. I hate to think that he might be growing up in poverty and obscurity.

You may ask why I do not advertise publicly to find the woman Frank married. If I do, I am afraid that false claimants may come forward. And this may still happen, even after my death… see… letter from…

So I have taken steps… does not fall into the wrong hands. There is a considerable amount… concealed… place that you know well. I trust you, Charles, to ensure…

… may not have many years left to me. And my memory… fading terribly…

That was all I could make out. The writing had become a pale smudge, fading away like the old Earl's memories.

"Well!" I said. "If only we could have read the whole letter!"

"It still might not help much," said Luke. "He mentions a 'place you know well', but he doesn't actually name it."

80

"Who was Charles, I wonder?"

"Sounds like a friend from long ago," said Dylan.

"But when the Earl disappeared, his friends tried to find him," I said. "This Charles person obviously didn't come looking in the old hiding place, or he'd have found the letter."

"Maybe he was dead too," said Dylan. "There seems to be a lot of it about."

"So, where do we go from here?" said Luke. "Any ideas?"

Chapter 13:
Digging

"We should dig all around here," said Dylan. "Why didn't I think of bringing a spade?"

"I can borrow one of my dad's," I said.

Just my luck – when I got to the tool-room, Dad was there. I asked if I could take a spade, and he wanted to know why.

"To dig for treasure," I said quite truthfully. He laughed.

"All right, but make sure you bring it back here afterwards."

"The treasure?"

"The spade. It's worth more than any treasure you're likely to dig up."

He wouldn't be so helpful if he knew who would be using the spade. He had told me to keep away from Dylan. For a moment I felt guilty. He was my father and I ought to obey him. But then I forgot about him in the excitement of the search.

We took turns in digging around the fountain. It was tough work, for the ground was hard and dry. All we managed to dig up was earth, stones and plant roots.

Then the blade of the spade struck metal. With all my strength, I dug down further.

"Oh. It's only an old pipe."

I had uncovered what must be the water supply to the fountain. I flung the spade down in disgust.

Giving up on the fountain, we went further into the woods. But it was hard to decide where we should start digging. Luke got excited when he found a heap of earth beside a hole in the ground.

"That's a badger's sett," I said.

"So? It could still be the secret place the Earl was writing about."

"No it couldn't. It's only been there since last year."

"This is hopeless," said Dylan. "We can't dig up the entire wood."

Luke said, "I don't think the treasure is anywhere near here. I think we should be searching inside the Hall."

"My mum won't let you do that," I said.

"Then you have a go, Rebecca. She'll let you in, won't she?"

"I suppose so," I said reluctantly. I didn't think that treasure-hunting would be much fun on my own. "If you give me that key, I'll see if I can unlock anything with it."

"What are we going to do with the letters?" asked Dylan.

I said, "Leave them with me. That historian woman is supposed to be coming back to take some photos. I could show them to her and see what she says. And I might let my mum look at them, too. She knows the Hall better than anybody."

Mum was quite interested. She said I could look around for secret hiding places inside the Hall, but I must be very careful not to damage anything.

"You should stick to the parts of the building that are still the same as they were in the old Earl's day," she said. "That means the cellar, the second floor and the attics. Oh, and the Library. I don't think that was modernised when they did the rest of the ground floor."

The cellar! I hadn't even thought of looking there. And to be honest, I didn't like the idea. It was cold and dark and rather spooky… not to mention full of spiders.

"Would you come with me into the cellar?" I said.

"If I can find the time," she said. "I'm glad you've found something to do. You're missing your books, aren't you?"

"Yes," I said, feeling guilty again. I wasn't missing my favourite ones. I'd hid them at the Folly before Dad burned all the others on a bonfire.. But it was true, I missed having new books to read. Dad wouldn't let me bring home books from the town library, although a few months ago he wouldn't have minded that.

What was going to happen next? Were the rules going to get tougher and tougher? I felt as if we were marooned on a tiny island, surrounded by a dangerous sea. And the waters were rising. The island was shrinking all the time, crowding us closer together, restricting our lives.

★ ★ ★

Next morning, for a while, I helped Mum with polishing the furniture, so that she would have time to help me later on. Then I left her to it and went exploring.

First of all I tried the second-floor bedrooms which opened off the Hall of Mirrors. I tested the key in various keyholes, but it didn't fit any of them. Then I tapped the walls, unfolded the window shutters, and even tried to look up the chimneys. There was a fireplace in every room, but no central heating, unlike downstairs.

I thought of the armies of servants who used to run this place, carrying coal up the endless stairs, cleaning grates, emptying chamber-pots, dusting and sweeping and polishing. Surely, if there was a secret hiding place, the servants would have known about it too? But servants and masters were all gone long ago, and the secret with them.

As I went from one room to another, my own reflection flickered past me in the Hall of Mirrors. I stopped to look. The ancient glass was distorted, one panel making my face look too wide, another too narrow. Tall or short, fat or thin, ugly or pretty – which was the real me?

Sometimes I felt as if I didn't know who I was. When I saw myself reflected in the eyes of other people, the image kept changing. Good member of the Meeting or stupid Scarf Sister; quite friendly or hopelessly shy; loving daughter or secret rebel... who was I? Was there a real person somewhere inside all this?

And suddenly I thought of Lorna Marshall. Perhaps she had glanced in these mirrors as she went about her work. She might have seen her own face where mine was now, in her plain housemaid's cap, with the glittering, gleaming Hall of Mirrors around her.

She must have wondered who she was and where she belonged. Housemaid or noblewoman? A servant obeying orders, or the wife of a future Earl? And had she really loved Frank, or simply longed to escape the hard life of a servant? It was so long ago, there was no way of knowing.

I went downstairs, glad to get away from all those mirrors. Mum had mentioned the Library, so that was where I went next. It was a big room with bookshelves all around, stretching right up to the high ceiling. There was a moveable stepladder, so that you could get to the upper shelves.

It should have been my idea of heaven – hundreds of books that I had never read. But they all looked so old. Their brown leather spines were worn and faded; they gave off a dry, dusty smell. They had titles like *Half a Lifetime in Southern India, 1817-1853.*

Ignoring the books, I went around looking for keyholes and hiding places. Perhaps, if you knew the secret, a whole section of bookshelves would open up. And then what... a hidden room? A spiral staircase leading into unknown depths?

As I worked my way into the far corner, a book title caught my eye. Surely there was something not quite right about it? *Travels in the Peaks of Norfolk, 1878.* That was odd. Norfolk was very flat, I seemed to remember reading somewhere.

And next to it was *The Eight Wives of Henry VI*. Strange – very strange. Then *Treasure Highland... Around the World in 80 Years... Oliver Twitch...* All these books were fakes! When you tried to take them out of the shelves, they wouldn't move. But they must be here for a reason – to hide something?

Full of excitement, I ran my hands up and down, left and right. Under a shelf I felt a wooden handle, and I pulled it.

Two shelves of false books swung towards me at eye level, almost hitting me on the nose. Behind was a black metal door marked *Wiseman Safes*. It had a keyhole. But once again my key didn't fit..

"Ah, I wondered if you would find the safe," Mum said from over my shoulder.

"You knew about it!" I said, feeling let down. "Do you have a key to open it?"

"Yes, but it's not locked. It's empty."

The metal door creaked open, showing a small safe, quite empty apart from a thin layer of dust. I was bitterly disappointed, ready to give up treasure hunting for the day, or maybe forever.

"What about the cellar?" Mum suggested. "I can come with you now, if you like."

"Oh, all right. I bet we don't find anything, though."

"You never know," said Mum. "But we can't spend too long down there. That Hannah woman is supposed to be coming this afternoon."

"Is she? You never said."

"No, because I thought it's best if your dad doesn't know about it beforehand."

"Why?" I said, mystified. "He can't stop her coming to the Hall if Miss Morton says she can."

"I want to talk to her in private," said Mum. "So don't say a word about it, Rebecca."

All these secrets. All these lies. Surely this wasn't how God meant people to live? But I said nothing.

We went into the passage by the kitchen. Mum selected a key from her big keyring and unlocked a door. A worn brick staircase led down into the chill darkness of the cellar. I definitely wouldn't have gone down there on my own. It was the sort of place where, in a story, the door would swing shut and trap you inside…

Mum clicked a switch, and a feeble light came on at the foot of the stairs. "Come on," she said, "we haven't got all day."

It would be all right if Mum was there… wouldn't it?

Of course it would. Nothing to worry about. I followed her down the cracked, uneven steps.

Chapter 14:

Breaking rules

The main rooms of the house could have held a giant; the cellar seemed designed for Narnian dwarfs, or possibly hobbits. It was a maze of small rooms with low ceilings. There was a damp, mouldy, underground sort of smell.

We went into the black, dusty coal-hole, and the wine cellar with its rows of empty racks. There was a cool-room with marble slabs – no fridges or freezers in the old days. And a boiler-room, silent because the central heating was turned off for the summer. And several other nameless rooms and cupboards, mostly empty. None of them had locks that matched the mysterious key.

I tried to do the Sherlock Holmes thing, looking for rooms that didn't fit. But it was difficult down here because all the walls were so thick. They had to be, to hold up the weight of the building above. If one of those thick walls was hollow, how would you ever know?

After a while, Mum said she would have to go back upstairs – Hannah was due to arrive. "But you can stay here, if you want," she offered.

"No thanks," I said, shivering in the chill air.

As we made our way back towards the stairs, all the lights went off. In the total blackness, I grabbed Mum's arm. I felt a scream rising in my throat.

But my terror only lasted for a few seconds. The lights flickered back into life, dazzlingly bright after the darkness.

Mum said, "There must be a loose connection somewhere. The wiring down here is ancient. It should be rewired really, but I don't suppose I'll be around to see that happen." And she sighed.

"What do you mean, Mum?" For a horrible moment I thought she was talking about her own death. Was she ill, like Luke's sister?

"I mean, if I have to give up my job," she said.

I thought about this. "Would you miss the job, Mum? Sometimes you seem fed up with it."

"Well, yes, I do get fed up sometimes. But it would be even worse if I was stuck at home all day. And then, if we had to move…"

"Would we really have to move house?" I said, alarmed. "I like our house. And I love the gardens and the woods. Surely, if Dad was still the gardener here, we wouldn't have to move?"

"Well, he might not do that job forever." She lowered her voice. "Don't tell him I mentioned this. He's still making up his mind about it. Mr Fairweather – Lois's father – you know he's the manager of a factory? He's offered your dad a job."

"But Dad would hate that! He likes being out of doors. And where would we live?"

"That's part of the offer. There's a sort of granny flat at the Fairweathers' house. We could live there. It's not much smaller than where we are now. The Chosen Prophet says – ".

"Mum, I don't care what the Chosen Prophet says! I don't want to live in Lois Fairweather's house! And I bet you don't either."

"No," she admitted. "But it's up to your father to decide."

There was no time to talk about it, for Hannah Conway had arrived. I pushed the thought of moving to the back of my mind. Maybe it wouldn't happen. If it did, I decided I would run away and live at the Folly, like the old Earl.

While Hannah went around taking photographs of the Hall, I went to get the letters we'd found at the fountain. She was so interested that she put down her camera to read them.

"Do you have any idea who the Earl was writing to – this Charles person?" I asked her.

"It could be a childhood friend of his, Charles Lamont. They were both educated at Eton, and in the holidays Charles often came to stay at Mallenford Hall because his family were out in India. They kept in touch by letter all through their lives."

"Have you read the other letters?" I asked eagerly. "Does he mention a secret hiding place in any of them?"

"I don't think so, but I'll read them again and check."

"And why did Charles never find the letters at the fountain?"

"I believe Charles Lamont died in the Spanish flu epidemic of 1919. Perhaps the news hadn't reached the Earl when he wrote that letter. Or perhaps he did know, but he forgot."

"Will you let us know if you find any hints in the Earl's letters?" I asked her.

"Yes, of course."

She also looked at the key. "I'm no expert on keys, but I'd say it's probably not a door key. It looks as if it would fit a box or a chest of some kind. I'll see if the letters make any mention of that."

Mum went around with Hannah while she took some more pictures. I would have followed them, but Mum shooed me away. I remembered what she'd said about a private talk with Hannah.

The indoor photography seemed to take ages. At last Mum and Hannah came back to the entrance. Mum was looking happier than she had for ages. What had she wanted to talk about? I couldn't begin to guess.

★ ★ ★

Dad was happy too. He'd heard rumours that he might be asked to become an Elder. I couldn't understand why he liked the thought of this – it just meant more meetings to go to. He had been invited to another special Meeting in Bristol. He wouldn't be back until Monday morning.

On Sunday, Mum and I went to the usual three Meetings, early morning, mid-morning and afternoon. I thought Mum was acting a bit oddly – nervous, almost, as if she was keeping a secret.

As we drove back from the third Meeting, I thought she had taken a wrong turning.

"Where are we going, Mum?"

"Promise not to mention this to your dad, Rebecca. We're going to visit Hannah, and she's going to take us to her church."

"What?"

"You heard me. Promise not to tell?"

I nodded. Although I was bored by the thought of another religious service – my fourth of the day – I couldn't help feeling curious. Why had Mum decided to break the rules like this? And what would Hannah's church be like?

I liked Hannah's flat as soon as I walked in, because it was full of books. There was a cat curled up on the sofa – I'd often thought I would love to have a pet, but the rules didn't allow it. I saw a TV and a computer, too. Mum looked at those and turned away quickly.

We had tea with Hannah. We were breaking the rules in a big way! Actually having a meal with someone from outside the Meeting! I could tell that Mum felt guilty about it, but I didn't. I was enjoying myself.

At the same time I wondered why Hannah was being so kind to us. We hardly knew her. We didn't belong to her church or her family.

Suddenly I had a nasty thought. Maybe she was after the treasure! Dad said that worldly people cared about nothing except money. Perhaps she thought she could use us to find the Mallenford millions for herself.

But she didn't even mention that. She was talking about the church service. "It won't seem much like a Meeting," she warned us. "It's quite informal. We meet in a school, not a church building. And you might feel that the music's rather loud. If you really hate it and want to leave, just tell me."

At our Meetings, there were never any musical instruments – all we had was our voices. If the person who led the hymn singing started on the wrong note, the hymn got high and squeaky or low and growly. And all the hymns were old and mournful-sounding.

It was different at Hannah's church. There were drums and guitars playing loud, lively music – not like hymns at all. I liked the sound of it, although I didn't join in because I didn't know any of the songs. Mum stood silent beside me, looking as if she wasn't enjoying this much.

Then came the sermon, and I got ready to be bored for an hour or so. Amazingly, I found myself actually listening to what the preacher said. (And the preacher was a woman! That would never happen at a Meeting.)

As well as speaking, she used a white-board on the wall of the school hall. The first thing that came up was a question: *Who does God love the most – good people or bad people?*

I thought the answer was obvious. But she went on to talk about the "good people" in the time of Jesus – the teachers of the Law, who obeyed every word of the Old Testament. They criticised Jesus because he mixed with "bad people", outcasts and sinners. He even ate with them. How dreadful!

A strange thought came to me. These teachers sounded just like the Elders of the Meeting! Would the Elders have criticised Jesus, if they had met him? Too friendly with unbelievers… doesn't keep all the rules… not good enough…

The preacher said, "Jesus told these people a story about a man with 100 sheep. One of them wanders off and gets lost. Does he just forget about it? No – he loves each one of his sheep and doesn't want to lose any of them. He leaves the 99 obedient sheep in the field. He goes looking for the lost one. At last, far away, he hears it bleating."

A picture came up on the white-board. It showed a sheep caught in a prickly bush, and a man trying to untangle it, not caring about the thorns that hurt his hands.

And suddenly I thought: that's me. I'm just like that sheep, all tangled up. I can never free myself. I need help…

The preacher was still talking. "The shepherd is so pleased when he finds it! He lifts it onto his shoulders and carries it back home. Then he calls his friends and neighbours together, and they all help him to celebrate finding the lost sheep."

Of course, I had heard this story many times. I knew it by heart. But somehow I had never really *thought* about it. The shepherd, of course, was meant to be Jesus. I knew that too.

Another picture showed the face of the shepherd as he carried the sheep safely home. I liked how the artist had painted him, strong and yet gentle, with smiling eyes. He looked like someone you would like to meet.

Was that really what God was like? Not a strict teacher watching out for rule-breakers, but a good shepherd who loved all of us, his sheep?

"Maybe you feel a long way from God tonight," the preacher went on. "You know you've done things that are wrong. You think you could never be good enough to please God. And it's true – you can't make yourself good enough. None of us can. That's why Jesus came to save us. He gave his life for us. He took the punishment that we deserve, so we can go free.

"If you would like to know him, this is his promise. He says, *Here I am! I stand at the door and knock. If anyone hears my voice and opens the door, I will come in and eat with him.*"

Yes, Lord! I would like to know you. I am opening the door... come in.

Chapter 15:

Scared of spiders

I felt quite strange as we left the school hall. It was as if I'd been carrying a heavy weight for so long that it had almost become part of me. But now the weight had been taken away. I felt free! I felt like dancing!

Dancing. That's against the rules, said a cold, disapproving voice in my head.

I don't care about the rules! Rules can't save you. Only God can save you... thank you, God. Thank you, God.

Mum said to me, "You look very happy. Did you like Hannah's church?"

"Oh, yes. I wish we could go there all the time, instead of the Meeting."

I knew, even as I said this, that it would be impossible. Dad would never allow it. Maybe we could sneak back there when he was away, hoping that no one saw us...

Then suddenly I had a feeling that we were being watched. I looked around and saw a big car waiting at the traffic lights. It was the Fairweathers' car. Lois was in the back seat, staring out at us. She must be wondering why we were coming out of a school on a Sunday evening. A school with a bright yellow banner on the railings – *Welcome to Mallenford Free Church*.

The lights changed and the big car drove away. Mrs Fairweather, who was driving, didn't seem to have noticed us. But Lois had definitely seen us.

I was sure she would tell on us, because Lois always liked getting other people into trouble. Maybe it made her feel good. But she must have decided to keep quiet, for several days passed by quite peacefully. Dad came back from the special Meeting in an excellent mood, and nothing happened to change it.

I was in a good mood too. I had always felt as if God was far away, high up in heaven looking down on me. But now I knew he was close. He had come into my life because I had asked him to. I could talk to him as easily as to a friend.

All those years and years of Meetings had never made me feel this close to God. As Luke had said, the rules and restrictions were like an empty house, kept clean and tidy, but with no one living inside. It was different now.

Even Dad noticed my happiness. He asked if I was enjoying my school holidays. I said yes, wondering if I should tell him what had really happened. But I chickened out. I didn't want to make him angry.

Half way through the week, Lois called me. She started whining about how bored and fed-up she was. After a few minutes I felt just as bad. Boredom must be catching, like flu.

"I hate the holidays. There's nothing to do," she said. "Can I come over to your house?"

Desperately I tried to think of an excuse. But before I could come up with one, Lois said, "I saw you last Sunday outside you-know-where. Do you think I should tell my dad?"

"No! Don't do that. Of course you can come over, Lois. I'll just check with my mum."

Mum looked worried when I explained what was happening. She said, "Try to keep her happy, Rebecca. Tell her she can come over. It will only be for a couple of hours, after all."

So, next morning, Lois arrived in the big car. Mrs Fairweather got out too.

"I wonder if you could do me a favour," she said to Mum. "I need to buy new shoes for the three little ones. It would be so much easier if... do you think you might look after Simon for me?"

Simon was Lois's brother, a year younger than she was. I didn't like him much, from what I'd seen of him. He was always teasing his little sisters and picking arguments with Lois.

Mum said, "Actually, I am supposed to be at work. There's a man coming to service the boiler at the Hall."

Mrs Fairweather raised her eyebrows. "Are you still working, then? After what the Chosen Prophet said?"

"He gave us three months," said Mum. "I haven't handed in my notice yet."

"Mum's hoping he might change his mind," I said.

Lois's mum looked shocked. "That will never happen. *The word of the Lord abides for eternity.*"

Yes, but is the Chosen Prophet really hearing the word of the Lord? I wanted to ask. He could get things wrong. Even in the Bible, people got things wrong sometimes.

But I didn't dare to say it. If Mrs Fairweather's eyebrows went up any higher, they might vanish into her hair, never to be seen again.

She said to Mum, "Well, if you *have* to work, couldn't you take my two up to the Hall with you? I know they'll be interested to see the place, and I promise they won't be any trouble. Lois will keep Simon in order."

Lois made a face. Simon glowered at her.

"All right," Mum said. She didn't really have any choice about it.

Was this what it would be like if we lived in the Fairweathers' house? Would Mum be expected to act as an unpaid childminder for all those kids? And the Fairweathers would notice everything we did. We would never be able to visit Hannah or her church again.

The rules of the Meeting would close in on us. People would be watching us all the time. We would be trapped inside a maze, like the fairground House of Mirrors that Luke had described. We'd have to go round and round, always trying to look good in front of other people. Always wondering if our image looked right. Never managing to escape into freedom.

Please, God, show us a way to avoid that... please don't let Dad agree to move there...

★ ★ ★

While Mum was taking the boiler man down to the cellar, Simon ran off. Mum had told us all to stay on the ground floor, but Simon wasn't listening. He went charging up the grand staircase like an escaped monkey making for the treetops.

"Come on," I said to Lois. "We'd better keep an eye on him. If he breaks anything, Mum will be in trouble."

He went right up to the second floor and into the Hall of Mirrors. Here, even Simon stopped to stare for a second or two. We caught up with him, and Lois grabbed his arm.

"Wow! What is this place?" she said, looking around.

Simon said, "Is that real gold? Must be worth a lot of money."

"No, it's gold paint," I said, showing him a chipped place on the skirting where the wood showed through. At once he started kicking at it, trying to get some more paint to come off.

"Stop that," said Lois. "I'll tell Mum! I will!"

"*I'll tell Mum! I will!*" Simon mocked her. "Then I'll tell her about you breaking that blue vase last week."

"If you do, I'll kill you."

"Oh shut up, both of you," I said. "I used to think it would be nice to have a brother or sister. You're shattering all my illusions."

Simon wandered over to the window, looking out at the woods, the hill and the Folly. "Is that a real castle?" he asked.

"No." I explained about the Folly, but before I'd finished, Simon interrupted.

"What's that sort of sunken bit? There, look. Going up the hill."

He was pointing at something I had never noticed before. Maybe I had never looked at it from this distance. In the broad, grassy path that led up the slope, there was a slight depression, or perhaps a line of slightly darker-coloured grass. It ran towards the Folly, but faded out before reaching it.

"It's just a path, stupid," said Lois. "Where people's feet have trodden the ground down."

"Then why does it start half way up the hill?" said Simon. "And why does it stop before the castle? Answer that, stupid."

"Don't call me stupid, stupid."

"You started it, triple stupid. Stupid to the power of 3. Ha! She doesn't even know what that means. She really is stupid."

Lois hit him; he hit her back. Lois stumbled sideways, dangerously close to a gilded lamp-stand.

Something was going to get broken if they went on like this.

"Stop it!" I said sharply. "If you both shut up and listen, I'll tell you about the secret passage."

I didn't tell them anything important. I only talked about what Mrs Dawkins had mentioned ages ago – the old tale about a tunnel between the Hall and the Folly. Even Mrs Dawkins didn't believe it. But it might take their minds off trying to murder each other.

Simon said, "If there really is a secret passage, it must come into the house somewhere underground. So... is there a cellar?"

"Yes," I said. "Want to have a look?"

The cellar door was open and the light was on. The boiler man must still be down there, and probably Mum was, too. I didn't feel too scared about going in. Even if the lights went off again, we wouldn't be on our own down there. But just to be on the safe side, I got a torch from a kitchen cupboard and put it in my pocket.

We wandered through the passages and interconnecting rooms. After a while, Simon said, "Which way are we facing? I mean, which part of the cellar is nearest to the Folly?"

I couldn't answer that. I had to go back to the stairs and reset my sense of direction, for there were no windows down here.

Now I knew which way led towards the back of the building. We went as far as we could in that direction, reaching a good-sized room with a large wooden table in it. The table must have been built down here, for it was far too big to be carried down the cellar steps. Maybe this was the old kitchen where the servants used to eat their meals long ago.

There were several doors in the far wall. I knew they only led to some walk-in cupboards – I had checked them out the other day, with Mum. But I let Lois and Simon explore them. There wasn't much to see except empty shelves and a few mouse droppings.

"Look what I've found, Simon!" called Lois.

She held out her cupped hands, opening them suddenly to show a big spider. I screamed. Simon screamed even louder. The spider fell off Lois's hand and scuttled away.

"Ha ha! He's scared of spiders," said Lois triumphantly. "Ever since he ate one when he was two years old."

"She fed it to me," Simon said. "I was only a baby and she fed me a spider." He looked as if he might be sick just thinking about it. More and more, I felt glad to be an only child.

There was one more cupboard. Simon disappeared inside it, and we heard him knocking on the walls.

"Hey! I think it sounds hollow!" he cried.

"Where? Let me see," said Lois.

"There, look. Down below that shelf. Right in the corner."

He slid out of the way, letting Lois and me into the cupboard. Lois tapped on the wall.

"What are you talking about? It sounds perfectly normal to me," she said.

Suddenly the cupboard door swung shut. I tried to stick my foot in the opening – too late. It closed, and I heard a bolt slide across on the outside. Simon had locked us in the cupboard!

Furious, I banged on the door. "Simon! Don't be an idiot! Let us out!"

He was shouting something that I couldn't hear very well because Lois was screaming her head off. Something about scared of the dark – serve her right...

I remembered the torch and switched it on. It gave a dim, yellow light... the battery must be dying. But the light was enough to stop Lois screaming. Or maybe she had no breath left.

She clutched my arm, digging her fingers in like claws. Her breathing came in funny little gasps. Was this what people called a panic attack?

"Simon, this isn't funny!" I yelled. "Open the door!"

No answer. The door of the kitchen slammed shut. Simon went away and left us locked inside.

Chapter 16:

The door

For a while I shouted and banged on the door, but nobody came. It was an old door, solid and thick, and the kitchen door was probably the same. No one was likely to hear us unless they came right into the room.

I stopped shouting because my voice was getting hoarse.

"It's all right," I said to Lois. "Don't worry. As soon as my mum realises we've disappeared, she'll come looking for us."

I was wondering, though, how long it would be before she missed us. Would we run out of air to breathe? No, for the door wasn't a very tight fit. I could see a thin line of light beneath it, so the air must be able to get in too.

But I had begun to realise something. I didn't like being shut in like this. Lois was scared of the dark – I was scared of that shut-in feeling. I once read a horror story where the walls of the room were pressing in, closer and closer, squeezing and crushing you...

Oh God, help us!

"Where's your mum? Why isn't she coming?" Lois said in a trembling voice.

"Give her a chance! We've only been here a few minutes. And she was busy with the boiler man. Sooner or later she'll wonder where we are."

Or would she? The Hall was so big, she might think we were upstairs or out in the garden. Simon might tell her we'd gone back to the Lodge. She might waste a lot of time looking in all the wrong places.

I said, "Lois, I'm going to switch the torch off for a while." (If I didn't, the battery would soon be dead, but I didn't want to tell her that.) "We don't really need it. There's a bit of light coming in under the door – see?"

I switched it off. Lois crouched down on the floor, as if to get closer to that thin strip of light, no broader than a matchstick. She was starting to shake again.

"I hate the dark. I hate the dark," she muttered, on and on, like somebody trapped inside a nightmare. "I hate it! I'm going to get Simon for this!"

"If only you hadn't shoved that spider under his nose," I said.

Suddenly she screamed again. The line of light had disappeared. We were left in total darkness.

What had happened? Had the faulty electric supply failed again? Or had Mum turned the lights off, thinking the cellar was empty, and locked the upper door?

Quickly I switched the torch back on. Lois was really panicking now. She was yelling like mad. She kicked the door and beat on it with her fists.

"Lois. Lois! Stop that! It's not helping!"

She didn't seem to hear me. She kicked out wildly, catching me on the ankle. Trying to avoid her, I climbed up the shelves at the side, using them like a ladder.

Maybe Lois kicked something. Maybe I touched some hidden catch. All I knew was, I felt a movement. The whole rear wall of the cupboard swung away from me, like a door opening. I was so shocked, I almost dropped the torch.

"Lois, we found it. The secret door! Look! Lois, will you STOP THAT?"

At last I got through to her. She stopped yelling. She turned to look at the dark space which had opened up at the back of the cupboard.

I shone the torch into the gap. Its dim light showed a narrow passageway with brick walls and a low, arched ceiling. You couldn't see where it led – the light didn't reach that far. It looked dark and ancient, damp and cold as a grave.

Lois gazed at it. "Can we get out that way?"

"How should I know?"

"You said the passage went to that Folly place."

"That's what Mrs Dawkins said, but she didn't really know. And I've never found another entrance at the Folly. I spent ages looking, once."

I was afraid that we might get all the way along the passage and be unable to get out at the far end. And the torch battery might not last much longer. That would be horrible – to be lost in the tunnel, in the dark. But then, if the torch died on us, it wouldn't be much fun in the cupboard either.

I said, "I don't think we should go in there. We should wait for my mum to find us."

"But that might take ages! And the torch battery might run out." Her voice was trembling again. "Can't we at least see where the passage goes to?"

I was about to say no. Then I remembered something – the treasure. Could it be that the Earl had hidden his money in the tunnel? Suddenly it didn't seem so dark and forbidding.

"All right. But we'd better fix this door open somehow. I don't want to get trapped inside the tunnel."

A couple of bricks lay on the floor of the tunnel. You could see the gap where they'd fallen from the ceiling arch. I used them to prop the secret door open, making sure it couldn't swing shut. Then we set off.

The tunnel was too narrow for us to walk side by side. I went in front because I had the torch. Lois, holding onto my arm, was so close behind me that we nearly tripped each other up.

That horrible shut-in feeling had not left me. The arched ceiling was so low that I had to bend my head. The tunnel walls seemed as close together as the sides of a coffin. The torchlight only reached a few feet ahead of me – beyond was darkness.

We seemed to be going uphill. That was good, I thought. Maybe we really would come out at the Folly.

"Are we nearly there yet?" whispered Lois.

"I don't know."

Instead of a stone floor, there was now earth underfoot... earth and rocks. It looked as if part of the ceiling had collapsed onto the floor. I began to wonder what would happen if a section fell down while we were underneath it. We might be crushed beneath fallen bricks and earth.

"Lois, I don't think this is safe. We ought to go back."

"No! No! I don't want to. Go on," Lois said, pushing me from behind.

The piled-up earth made the space inside the tunnel even smaller. Soon I had to get down on my hands and knees. The torchlight showed only darkness around us, with plant roots pale against the black soil. I felt as if I was inside a foxhole, not a man-made tunnel.

Oh, God, help me. What should I do? Go on or go back? What if the roof meets the floor and we can't go any further? I don't want to get stuck here... help me!

The gap began to open up again. In the failing light of the torch, I could see a proper roof and floor, like before. Soon I could stand up again.

Lois grabbed my arm; I could feel her shivering. "That wasn't very nice," she said.

"Come on. Don't stop," I said, for the light was very dim now.

We hurried on, feeling as if we had walked for miles. At last I could make out some narrow stone steps leading upwards. I went up eagerly, with Lois close behind.

At the top, I could just see a low ceiling of stone. It must be moveable, surely? There must be a way out, or what was the use of the tunnel?

I heaved against it with all my strength. Nothing happened.

"What's the matter?" said Lois.

"There's a stone blocking the way! I can't shift it!"

"Let me try."

Both of us pushed as hard as we could, but the stone did not move. It must be very heavy, or maybe it was cemented in place. We had come to a dead end.

The last of the torchlight faded and left us in the dark.

Chapter 17:

Shut in

Before Lois could start screaming again, I grabbed her hand.

"Don't be scared. We can find our way back, even in the dark," I said.

"What if we get lost?"

"We won't. The tunnel was straight. It didn't branch at all. We just have to go down the hill, and soon we'll be back at the Hall, and Mum will come to find us."

"It's all right for you. Y-you're not scared of the d-dark," she said shakily.

I didn't tell her about my fear of being shut in. Maybe, if she thought I was brave and strong, she would try to be brave too.

But my skin crawled at the thought of the tunnel. The crumbling bricks and mortar, losing their strength... the walls closing in... the low roof with tons of earth and rock above it, ready to fall...

Oh God, help us! Oh God, help us!

With one hand on the wall, and the other clutching Lois's hand, I stepped blindly down the narrow stairway. At last we reached the bottom. The darkness was blacker than the darkest night. The stale-smelling air was silent and still.

Some words from the Bible ran through my mind. *The Lord is my shepherd... he makes me to lie down in green pastures...*

Not many green pastures here, I thought bitterly. But then, God didn't lead us here – we chose this path. We shouldn't have tried to save ourselves. We should have waited to be rescued.

He leads me in paths of righteousness... Though I walk through the valley of the shadow of death, I will fear no evil, for you are with me.

Are you still here with me, Lord? Here in the valley of the shadow? I shouldn't have come here – it was stupid. I know that now. But are you still with me?

Slowly, feeling my way forward, I went along the tunnel. Lois, behind me, was clutching my arm. I could hear her quick, shallow breathing. She sounded on the verge of panicking.

Now I was stepping on something that felt like soft earth We must be coming to that place where the roof had collapsed.

"Lois, this is where we have to crawl, remember? We have to get down on our hands and knees."

"No," she gasped. "No. I can't do it. Not in the dark."

"We have to. It's the only way back."

"I can't!"

"Well then, you stay here, and I'll go on. When Mum finds me we'll get a better torch and come back for you."

"I can't stay here on my own!" she cried.

Oh help. Now what? Can't go forward. Can't go back. Can't stay here. What do we do, Lord?

In the silence I began to hear a sound… a whispering sound, soft as sand trickling between my fingers. Small, invisible things were falling on me, like dry snowflakes. What was happening?

Run. Run back, said a voice in my head.

"Lois, go back!"

"Why? What's going on?"

"I don't know. Just get moving! Come on!"

I tried to push her back up the tunnel, but she wouldn't move. I squeezed past her, grabbed her hand, and started pulling her towards the stairs. We stumbled blindly up the hill.

From behind us came a rattling, rumbling noise that grew louder and louder. Terror exploded inside me.

A gust of air blasted us. I heard some heavy thumps, as if bricks were falling. Then the sounds died away into silence.

"What happened?" Lois gasped.

I said shakily, "I think some more of the roof fell in."

"Are… are you going to go back and see?"

"Don't be stupid," I said.

Nothing would have made me go back down that tunnel. I was still feeling the after-shocks of that terror… terror of being crushed and squeezed under falling rocks.

Trying to sound strong, I said, "I don't think it's safe. Another part might fall down. I think we should go back to the steps."

"And then what do we do?"

"What we should have done right at the start. Wait for my mum to find us."

Then I had a terrible thought. What if Mum was already looking for us? What if she found the secret door and started exploring the passage? It wasn't safe! But how could we tell her? We would just have to listen, listen carefully, and shout a warning if we heard anyone coming along the tunnel.

I sat down on the lowest step of the stairs. Straining my ears for any sound, I started praying again.

Help us, Lord. You're the only one who can help us…

It was cold, sitting there. The steps felt slimy and damp. There was nothing to hear, nothing to see in the black darkness.

Putting out my hand, I felt a sort of wooden ledge to one side of the passage. It made a better seat than the cold stone steps. We sat on it, side by side. I could feel Lois trembling.

"Are we going to run out of air to breathe?" she said.

"I don't know. There must be…"

I stopped in mid-sentence.

"There must be what?"

"Shhh. I'm listening."

There wasn't a sound from down the tunnel. But I thought I had heard something from above.

"Can you hear a noise?" I said to Lois.

"Yes! It sounds like footsteps – up there."

Still listening, we crept up the stairs. At the top, I could hear muffled voices.

"Help!" we both started yelling. I banged on the stone ceiling with the only thing I had – the torch. It broke in my hand, but I didn't care.

"Help us! Help!"

"Who's there?" That sounded like Dylan.

"It's me – Rebecca!"

"And me," shouted Lois. "We found the secret passage!"

"But we can't get out. We're trapped."

There were knocking and banging sounds from up above. Then Luke shouted, "We can't shift this stone. We need to get help."

"Find my dad," I called. "He'll know what to do."

They went away. And now there was a silence which seemed endless.

"I wish they would hurry up," Lois said.

"Me too."

What would Dad say when the boys arrived out of nowhere? He would probably be furious with them for being here. I just hoped he would listen to them and believe what they said.

"I wish we had one of those mobile phone things," I said.

I expected Lois to remind me that they were against the rules. She said, "They don't work in places like this."

"How do you know?"

She hesitated, then said, "My Dad's got one. Don't tell! He has to have it for his work. But if anyone finds out, he'll be put out of the Meeting."

"I won't tell, if you promise not to tell anyone about Mum and me going to church."

"Okay." She was silent for a moment. Then she said, "What I don't understand is, why did you want to go there?"

"Because it's not like the Meeting," I said. "For me, all these rules and things – they're like a dead end. Like this tunnel. They don't lead anywhere – they don't help you to know God."

"And going to church is different, is it?"

I found it hard to explain. It wasn't going to church that had made the difference. It was letting God into my life, talking to him, listening for his voice...

Suddenly I heard someone calling my name.

"Rebecca! Are you all right?"

"Dad!" I shouted.

"Don't worry. We'll soon have you out of there."

Heavy blows began to thud against the stone above us. Afraid that something might fall on us, we moved back down the steps.

There was a loud crack as the stone ceiling split in two. Part of it was lifted aside. Daylight – wonderful daylight – came into the darkness, and I saw Dad's face. I had never been so glad to see anyone in all my life.

Dad helped us to climb out. I realised that I was filthy, covered with mud, but he didn't care. His arms enfolded me in a huge hug. And I felt safe... safe at last.

Chapter 18:

Opening up

"Where are we?" asked Lois.

"In the Folly," said Luke.

"How did you boys get into the grounds?" Dad asked, his voice stern.

"Er… we climbed over a broken wall," said Dylan.

"That's trespassing. You were breaking the law."

"Dad! Don't get mad at them!" I cried. "If they hadn't been here, we would still be trapped in the tunnel."

I looked around. We were in one of the small, stone-floored rooms. In the corner was a gap in the floor, where Dad had broken one of the flagstones with his sledgehammer.

"No wonder we never found the way in," said Dylan. "It looked just like every other bit of the floor. We only knew where it was because we heard you shouting."

"Did you find the treasure?" Luke asked eagerly.

I shook my head. The money had been the last thing on my mind.

"I'll go down and check it out," said Luke.

"No, you won't," Dad said firmly.

I said, "It's not safe! The roof nearly fell in on us. And where's Mum? She hasn't gone into the tunnel, has she?"

"She's just coming," said Dad.

I looked out of the window. Mum, holding Simon firmly by the arm, was hurrying up the grassy path from the Hall.

"Mum, be careful," I shouted. "There's a tunnel under there and it might cave in. Don't walk on that sunken-in bit."

"Ah," said Dad. "I noticed that the last time I mowed the grass. I thought it could have been caused by the water pipe to that old fountain. Never guessed there might be a tunnel!"

We started telling him about the hidden door in the cellar. But suddenly Dylan said, "Hey! Where's Luke gone?"

"Down here," came a hollow-sounding voice.

"Luke!" I yelled. "Come out of there! I told you – it's not safe!"

"I've found something. A box," he shouted.

We looked through the hole in the floor. Luke was shining a light on the wooden shelf thing at the bottom of the steps. But it wasn't a shelf – it was a metal-bound wooden box with handles on the sides. It looked like something out of *Treasure Island*.

"I don't believe it," Dylan breathed.

I couldn't believe it either. Had Lois and I been sitting on the Mallenford Millions?

Dad, as interested as any of us, went down and helped Luke with the box. We all crowded round as they tried to open it.

"Locked," said Dad.

I said, "I'll get the key."

"What key?" Dad didn't know about the key or the letters we'd found.

"Explain to him, Dylan. I'll run and get it."

"No, tell me where it is and I'll get it," said Dylan. "You don't look as if you should be running anywhere."

"You should be getting in a hot bath," said Mum. "And so should Lois. I don't know what your mum will say when she sees you, Lois."

"Mum! Never mind that! We think we've found the Mallenford treasure!"

Dylan ran to the Lodge to get the key. (For once, Dad didn't say a word about him going into our house.) Meanwhile, we took the box down to the Hall. Dad and Luke lifted it onto the kitchen table.

When Dylan brought the key, it fitted easily into the heavy lock. But it wouldn't turn.

"The lock must have seized up," said Dad. "Maybe a bit of oil will loosen it." He went to get some from the toolroom.

Luke said, "There can't really be two million pounds in there. The box isn't big enough."

"There won't be two million," I said. "It was £50,000 that went missing. They only said it would have been worth the same as two million is worth nowadays."

"£50,000 is still a lot of money. But maybe it won't be worth anything at all," said Mum. "Don't get too excited."

Dad came back. He carefully oiled the lock and slid the key in. I could feel everyone in the room holding their breath.

This time the key turned. Dad lifted the lid.

"Oh," said Luke, disappointed. "It's only a load of old papers."

Carefully Mum took out one of the papers. It was white, with printing that curled like old-fashioned handwriting.

"*I promise to pay the bearer on demand the sum of ten pounds*. I think it's a ten pound note! Bank notes must have looked different in those days."

"Will they still be worth anything, though?" asked Dylan.

"I don't know."

We stared at the box of old money. There were thousands of the bank notes, but perhaps they were worthless, only good to light fires with.

"I tell you what," said Mum. "I'll ring Hannah – she'll know. And I must ring Miss Morton too. Meanwhile I'm going to put it all in the safe."

As she locked up the safe, a bell rang loudly, making me jump. I could see a car in the distance, outside the main gates. Mum pressed the electronic switch to open the gates.

Lois's family had come back from their shopping trip. Mrs Fairweather was not at all pleased to see Lois with her mud-spattered clothes and wind-blown hair. Lois's headscarf had vanished – it was probably somewhere in the tunnel. (I definitely wasn't going back to look for it.)

"What on *earth* have you girls been doing? How did you get into a state like that? Simon seems to have managed to stay quite clean for once."

"That's not fair! This is all Simon's fault!" Lois cried. "He locked us up in the cellar and we couldn't get out!" And suddenly she burst into tears.

"I wouldn't have done it if she hadn't shoved a spider in my face," Simon said. "I hate her!" He aimed a kick at Lois's ankle.

"Behave yourselves," Mrs Fairweather said coldly. Her accusing stare rested on each of us in turn. It even included Mum, saying silently, *You should have taken better care of my children.*

"Wait till your father hears about this," Mrs Fairweather said ominously. She hurried her children back to the car.

Mum said, "Now she'll go around telling everybody that I'm not a good mother. She'll say work is more important to me than my family."

"Mum, you shouldn't care about what they say," I said. "You *are* a good mother."

She hugged me. But I knew that my opinion wouldn't count for much against everyone else's. If almost every mirror in the room gives you a warped, ugly image of yourself, why should you trust the one good reflection?

★ ★ ★

That evening we had an unexpected visit from two of the Elders, Mr Glover and Mr Paulson. At first I thought they might have come to tell Dad he was being made an Elder. But their faces were too serious for that. They looked the way Dad looked at me when I'd done something wrong.

I was sent upstairs while they talked to Mum and Dad. But in our small house, where the stairs were part of the living-room, I could still hear most of what they said.

"Mary, is it true that you went to a church on Sunday?" Mr Paulson made it sound as if she'd gone to a wild party and come home drunk.

"Of course she didn't," Dad said, shocked. "Mary wouldn't do such a thing."

"I'm asking Mary, not you. And you needn't try to deny it, Mary. You were seen coming out of Mallenford Free Church on Sunday evening."

So Lois hadn't been able to keep her big mouth shut! I was furious. She must have known how much trouble she would cause us.

"And even worse," said Mr Glover, "you took your daughter there too. Leading your own child astray!"

"Mary," Dad said, "is this true?"

"Yes," said Mum in a low voice.

"And furthermore," Mr Paulson said, "you have not been walking in obedience. The Chosen Prophet has said that women shouldn't do paid work, but you are still doing it."

"You ought to have handed in your notice as soon as you heard the Chosen Prophet's ruling," said Mr Glover.

Without giving her a chance to say anything, they started attacking Dad. "James, you should have kept your wife in order. Why have you been letting her wander from the paths of righteousness?"

There goes Dad's chance of becoming an Elder, I thought to myself.

They went on and on, using Bible verses like sticks to beat Mum and Dad with. Dad tried to argue back, but they wouldn't let him get a word in edgeways. Mum said nothing at all.

The Elders wanted Mum to promise never to visit a church again. I expected her to agree meekly, whatever she felt inside. These were the Elders, after all. Only the Chosen Prophet was more important than they were.

But Mum, at last, spoke up. She said, "I can't make that promise."

"Why not?"

"Because I found something at that church that I've been missing for a long time. I felt the nearness of God."

"God is always near to us in the Meeting," said Mr Glover. "*Where two or three are gathered together unto my name, there am I in the midst of them.*"

Mr Paulson said, "And all the churches are full of pride and worldliness."

"How do you know that? You've never been to one." (Good one, Mum, I thought.)

"The Chosen Prophet has said it," said Mr Paulson. "So it must be true."

Mr Glover said, "You know what the Bible says. *Come out from the midst of them, and be separated, saith the Lord.*"

"If you go to that church again, you will be put out of the Meeting," Mr Paulson said sternly.

Mum said, "But it's just not true that everyone outside — "

"Are you trying to argue with the word of God?" demanded Mr Paulson.

"No, of course not. I believe in God's word. But I think the Chosen Prophet sometimes misunderstands it."

There was a shocked silence.

Dad said, "Mary! Think what you're saying! She doesn't really mean that – she's been upset lately — "

Mr Glover said, "If you don't accept the authority of the Chosen Prophet, you cannot be one of us."

"You will have to leave the Meeting," said Mr Paulson. "You'll split up your own family. That's an evil, sinful thing to do. How could you bear not to see your husband and daughter again?"

I couldn't stand any more of this. I ran down the stairs.

"It's not Mum who is evil! You're the ones who split up families, with your rules! If you make me choose between Mum and the Meeting, I'll go with Mum."

The look on Dad's face stopped me in my tracks. "I'm sorry, Dad. But can't you see how wrong they are to do this? Come with us. Come with Mum and me, and forget them all."

I ought to have known it would be useless. Dad couldn't suddenly forget everything he'd been taught all through his life. His face closed up like a locked safe.

"Leave them, James," said Mr Glover. "Perhaps Mary will come to her senses when she realises what she's done."

Mr Paulson stood up. "Yes, James, come with us. You can stop at my place. Don't stay in this house a minute longer! I can see she is a rebellious woman, and her child is like her."

Dad got up, still looking shocked, as if he didn't know what had hit him. Mum looked ready to cry.

Be brave, Mum. Don't give in to them, I wanted to whisper. I held her hand tightly.

"Mary, we withdraw our fellowship from you," said Mr Paulson. "You are no longer welcome at our Meetings. You must not speak to any of God's people."

"Until you agree that the Chosen Prophet is to be obeyed without question," Mr Glover said.

Mum said, "The Chosen Prophet is not God. He's only human! And I don't believe he is always right. As the Bible says, *We ought to obey God rather than men.*"

"We can't speak to you. We cannot hear you. We have withdrawn from you," Mr Paulson said loftily. "James! Come on."

Between them they shepherded Dad out of the room. He turned, as if he wanted to say something, but they didn't let him.

"Goodbye, James," Mum said softly.

"Someone will come over in a day or two to collect his belongings," said Mr Glover. "Make sure you have them ready."

I wanted to scream as Dad got into the car. I wanted to chase after him, but Mum held me back. Her hands were trembling. There was nothing we could do. We just stood there, watching them drive away.

Chapter 19:

How much?

Dad came back to the Hall the next morning to go to work. Mr Paulson dropped him off outside the gate and sat waiting while Mum let him in. Dad didn't speak to her or even look at her. Satisfied, Mr Paulson drove away.

As Dad walked up the drive, I ran after him. I had a question to ask him.

"Are you going to go on working here, Dad? Or will you take that job at Mr Fairweather's factory?"

He didn't answer me; he just walked on as if I wasn't there.

"Because Lois told me something. Her dad doesn't always keep the rules of the Meeting. He has a mobile phone that he uses for work. She told me not to tell anyone."

Why should I keep Lois's secret, when she hadn't kept mine? And I was ready to do anything in order to get Dad back. But Dad didn't react at all.

"Can't you see? It's all wrong! Those rules... they're not about pleasing God, just pleasing other people. Looking good. Not putting a foot wrong if people are watching, but breaking the rules in secret. Is that the way God wants people to live?"

He didn't even look at me. I felt powerless. I felt the way a ghost might feel in broad daylight, invisible, untouchable.

I said, "Dad, we really miss you. Mum was crying last night after you'd gone. I wish you would come back."

He spoke then. His voice sounded flat, empty of all feeling. "I can't come back. It would be against God's will. *Everyone who has left wife, or children, or lands, for his name's sake, shall inherit life eternal.*"

"What about *if I have all faith, so as to remove mountains, but have not love, I am nothing?* What about that, Dad?"

He turned away. He went into the toolroom and shut the door.

★ ★ ★

Miss Morton, the owner of the house, was supposed to be arriving that afternoon to see the tunnel and the treasure. Hannah was to be there too. I was glad they were coming – at least it took my mind off Dad.

I couldn't remember ever seeing Miss Morton before. Mum said that the last time she had visited the Hall, I was only five years old. When I tried to imagine what she would look like, I pictured a white-haired old lady like Miss Marple in the detective stories.

It was a shock to me when she arrived at the gate in a sports car. She was a smartly-dressed blonde woman who looked about 45. I knew that she had inherited the

Hall from her grandfather, along with a lot of money. Since then, although she had paid for the place to be looked after, she had never wanted to live in it.

As Mum unlocked the huge front door of the Hall, Miss Morton shivered a little. Then she laughed.

"You know, I used to be terrified of this place as a child," she said. "Someone must have told me it was haunted. When we came to visit my grandfather, I was always afraid that a ghost would jump out at me! And Grandfather was quite a frightening figure, too."

"My friend thought the Hall was haunted," I said. "He saw a picture on the Internet... but now we think it was just a reflection in a mirror."

While we waited for Hannah, I told her the story of Lorna and Frank. She was very interested.

"Perhaps, now that we've found what Lorna was looking for, her ghost will be able to rest," Miss Morton said.

I could see from Mum's face that she thought this was a silly idea, but she didn't say anything. After all, Miss Morton was her boss.

"Shall I open the safe and get the money out?" she asked.

By the time Hannah arrived, we had counted out all the notes into piles, weighing them down with books. There were 52 piles, each worth £1,000 – if they were worth anything at all.

"Is the money still usable?" I asked Hannah.

"Well, it wouldn't be accepted in a shop. If you took it to the Bank of England, you'd be given the face value – £52,000 in modern money. But it would probably be more valuable if it was sold to collectors. There are people who collect old bank notes as well as coins, and notes like these, in good condition, might be worth up to ten times their face value."

I did a quick sum in my head. £52,000 x 10... £520,000... over half a million pounds! Even Miss Morton was looking impressed.

"Who does it belong to?" she asked. "What happens now?"

"The first thing you must do is report the find within 14 days," said Hannah. "I can't say for certain, but I would expect the County Coroner to say that it's yours, Miss Morton. You are the landowner, and you hadn't given permission for anyone to look for treasure on your land."

"Oh," I said. "But the boy who found it... won't he get a reward? He really needs the money."

I told Miss Morton about Luke's sister, and the money that was needed to take her to America.

"He was really desperate to find the treasure," I said. "He kept on looking when Dylan and I got bored. He went down into the tunnel, even though it was dangerous. And if he hadn't, the treasure would still be down there."

Miss Morton said, "If it turns out that the money is mine, I'll make sure he gets a very good reward. But it sounds as if his family needs money right now."

"Yes," I said. "They do."

"Write down his name and address for me. I'll go and see him this afternoon."

We locked the money away again. Then we went up to the Folly, to see the place where it had been hidden for so long. The gap in the floor was still open, but nobody ventured in. I didn't even want to go near it.

"I wonder what I should do about the tunnel," Miss Morton said. "I have a feeling it might be expensive to repair the roof. Perhaps the safest thing would be to get it filled in."

"Oh, don't do that! It's part of the history of the Hall," said Hannah.

Mum said, "What I don't understand is, why would anyone bother to dig a tunnel like this?"

"Maybe they just thought it would make the Folly more interesting," I suggested. "They should have built a moat and a drawbridge, too."

But Hannah said, "There's some evidence that the first Earl of Mallenford was a secret supporter of the Jacobites. After the 1745 rebellion, when Bonnie Prince Charlie was defeated and escaped to France, many people hoped he would come back again. He sent secret agents to Britain and laid plans for another rebellion. All very dangerous... so perhaps the first Earl had the tunnel built as a secret way of escaping from the house."

"And the seventh Earl knew the secret," I said, "or maybe he found the tunnel when he was a boy. He thought it was a good place to hide his money."

"It was a very good place," said Miss Morton. "So good that nobody found it for nearly 100 years."

"And it only came to light because of Lois and a spider," I said. "It's funny how things work out."

* * *

After Miss Morton went away, Mum invited Hannah to come in for a cup of tea. She was quite free to do that now. There was nobody to forbid it.

Mum told Hannah what the Elders had said to us. Hannah knew exactly how we were feeling; she had been through the same thing when she was young. We talked for a long time.

"You mustn't think that you are alone in the world," Hannah said. "Call me whenever you want to. And come to church on Sunday if you feel ready to."

"Yes, I'd like that," Mum said, and I nodded.

I was just waking up to the fact that the rules of the Meeting didn't apply to us now. I wouldn't have to sit through three Meetings every Sunday. I could choose my own friends. I could wear what I liked – I could even get my hair cut!

But none of this made up for the fact that Dad wasn't there.

"How can we make Dad come back?" I asked Hannah.

She said, "You can't *make* him do anything. He probably misses you as much as you miss him, but he's under a lot of pressure right now. Pray for him. Pray that he'll find freedom."

She looked sad as she said it. I wondered if there were people in her own family who still belonged to the Meeting – people she hadn't seen for years.

Mum said, "I wish he could see that the Chosen Prophet might sometimes make a mistake. And that the Elders aren't always right, either."

"Jesus said, *I am the Good Shepherd*," said Hannah, "but he warned us that there are other shepherds who are not so good. They lead the sheep – that's us – the wrong way. And if a wolf comes, or danger threatens the sheep, the bad shepherds run away, and the sheep are scattered in all directions."

"It's better to follow the Good Shepherd," I said.

"Yes," said Hannah. "Keep on praying for your Dad. That's the best thing you can do for him right now."

Chapter 20:
More reflections

The finding of the Mallenford treasure made front-page news in the local paper. There were several pictures – the Folly, the tunnel entrance, and Luke with the money-box (empty by now, but you couldn't tell that from the photo).

After that, lots of people arrived at the gates of the Hall, wanting to come in and look around. Mum turned them away, telling them to come back on the Open Day. It looked like being the busiest Open Day we'd ever had.

Miss Morton, as she had promised, went to see Luke. She gave him a cheque for £10,000! That was more than enough for the trip to America. It meant that Luke could go along with his mother and sister. They hadn't had the money to take him the previous time.

"And she said that when everything is sorted out, she'll make sure that I get a lot more money," he said. "So I told her that you and Dylan deserved a reward too. I would never have found the treasure without you."

"What about Lois and her brother?" I said. "It was because of them that I found the tunnel. They deserve something, don't they? Like about 10p each."

A few days later I happened to see Lois in town. She was waiting outside a chemist's shop with two of her little sisters. I guessed her mum was inside the shop.

"Hi, Lois," I said, just to see if she would speak to me.

I don't think she recognised me straight away, because I wasn't wearing my Meeting clothes. Mum had actually let me buy some jeans. Amazing! I had never worn any kind of trousers in my life before.

And I'd had a proper haircut at a salon, instead of Mum just trimming the ends of my long hair. It was shoulder-length now. I really liked it.

When Lois realised that it was me, she stared and stared. She looked disapproving and yet envious. Then she glanced over her shoulder. There was no sign of her mum.

She said, "Do you think you'll ever come back to the Meeting?"

"No. At least I hope not."

"You are mean. I won't have anybody to sit with at lunchtime now."

I felt sorry for her. "We can still talk, Lois. Nobody's going to know what you do when you're at school."

"My brother will," she said gloomily. "He'll be starting at our school in September. If he sees us talking, he'll tell on me."

There was something I was desperate to find out. I still didn't know if Dad was going to go on working at the Hall – where at least I would see him every day, even if he wouldn't talk to me.

"Lois, can I ask you something? Is my dad going to work at your father's factory?"

"He *was* going to," Lois said. "But I don't know if he will now. There's been a big argument."

"A big argument? What about?"

"I don't really know. Dad won't tell me. But something weird is going on. Half the Elders aren't speaking to the other half."

"Really?"

She lowered her voice. "I think something happened at the last Special Meeting. My dad went to it, and he came back in a terrible mood. I don't think he's even told Mum what happened. But it must have been something bad."

"Lois! Come here!"

Mrs Fairweather's sharp voice jerked Lois away from me as if she was a dog on a lead. Looking guilty, she rounded up her little sisters and hurried off after her mother.

When we went to church on Sunday, Hannah had some more news.

"I had a phone call last night from a cousin I haven't seen in years," she said. "He's just left the Meeting, along with all his family. It's wonderful!"

"Why did he leave?" I asked.

Hannah explained, "He went to a Meeting to hear the Chosen Prophet speak. But the Prophet was acting very strangely, and after a while, people began to realise that he'd been drinking. In fact he was so drunk he was getting his words mixed up. And when they tried to get him off the platform, he started cursing and swearing. He hit one of the Elders and knocked him over!"

"So then what happened?" asked Mum.

"Well, they got him calmed down in the end, and the Elders warned everybody not to mention what had happened. They were trying to pretend that everything was all right. But my cousin had had enough. He had been wanting to leave for some time – that gave him a reason to go."

"Oh!" I said. "I wonder if Dad was at that Meeting?"

"Even if he was, it might not change anything," Mum warned me. "Don't get your hopes up."

* * *

Hannah had given me a modern version of the Bible. It was much easier to understand than the old-fashioned Meeting Bible. I read it quite often, even though I had all my favourite books at home now. I wasn't reading it because I'd been told to, but because I wanted to know more about God.

Wherever the Spirit of the Lord is, there is freedom. I liked that verse. Freedom – not struggling to keep to the rules. Not worrying about what other people thought of me. Not trying to be like everyone else.

We can see and reflect the glory of the Lord. And he makes us more and more like him as we are changed into his glorious image.

That made me think of the Hall of Mirrors, with all its weird, distorted images. We are meant to be better mirrors than those – we are meant to face the Lord and reflect his image truly. And he will make us more and more like himself...

As I was reading, I heard footsteps outside. Dad had arrived to go to work. Strange – he was carrying his suitcase. And suddenly my heart leapt. Had he decided to come back to us?

I ran to open the gate for him. But he didn't smile or even glance at me. He looked worried and upset. He trudged off along the drive.

"Dad!" I hurried after him. "Wait a minute!"

He stopped. Oh God, please give me the right words to say!

"Are you... did you go to the last Special Meeting?"

He nodded.

"Lois said there was a big argument or something. She said half the Elders aren't talking to the other half."

Dad said angrily, "The Chosen Prophet was drunk. From what people say, it isn't the first time. But they always managed to hush it up before now."

"Not this time, though," I said.

"No. And now the Meeting has split right down the middle. One lot are trying to pretend that nothing happened. The others say we should appoint a new Prophet. And I don't know who's right."

"Maybe they're both wrong," I said. "*We ought to obey God rather than men.*"

He stared at the ground. "I don't know how to do that any more. I don't know what God's will is."

Wearily, he picked up his suitcase.

"Why have you got your things with you, Dad?" I asked.

"I had an argument with Roy Paulson. I can't stay there any longer."

"Where are you going to sleep tonight, then?"

"In the toolroom, I suppose."

"Oh, Dad! Don't be like that!"

"Like what?"

"So… so proud and stiff. Come home. Come back to us."

He said uncertainly, "Do you think Mary would have me back?"

"I know she would."

I took his hand and led him home. And Mum came running to meet us.

★ ★ ★

Dad has changed. He's not so certain that he's right any more. He has stopped going to the Meeting. (It has split into two smaller groups which hate each other.) He still keeps many of the rules he's always lived by, but he doesn't force Mum and me to do the same.

We asked him to come to church with us, but he wouldn't.

"It's too soon," Mum said. "Give him time. Maybe one day..."

I keep asking Mum if I can have a TV. At the moment she is saying no. But she doesn't mind if I watch TV at a friend's house. And she says I can have a mobile phone, if I save up the money. We might get a dog... we might go on holiday... my whole life is changing.

There are changes, too, at Mallenford Hall. Miss Morton sometimes comes to stay for a few days at a time. She says that the atmosphere of the place has changed; she feels more at home here now. She might sell her London place and move here permanently. She also has plans to open the Hall for visitors more often.

"Extra work," Mum says with a sigh, but I know she is pleased really. It will be good to see the Hall being lived in, not sitting there empty and silent.

In the run-up to the Open Day, I helped Mum and Mrs Dawkins to clean the Hall of Mirrors. I stopped working when I saw my own reflection, which still had the power to surprise me. I didn't look like a Scarf Sister any more. The mirror showed an ordinary-looking girl in jeans and a T-shirt.

But I didn't feel like an ordinary girl. Maybe I would never fit in with the other girls at school. My whole upbringing had made me too different from them. I wouldn't care too much, though, as long as Dylan and Luke were my friends.

I'd had enough of struggling to fit in, trying to be a mirror image of other people. *We can see and reflect the glory of the Lord... he makes us more and more like him...*

"Come on, girl," said Mrs Dawkins. "Don't spend all day admiring yourself. How about making us a nice cup of tea?"

I made some tea and we all sat down to drink it together – another thing we wouldn't have done a few months ago. In the middle of this, someone rang the bell at the gate. It was Hannah.

"I wanted to show you the proposed cover of my book," she said, "and see what you thought."

Dad, Mum and I were on the cover! Hannah had taken a photograph of the Hall from the end of the drive. And there we were, three small figures by the front door.

"It adds a bit of human interest," she said. "Of course you'll be mentioned in the book, when I write about the tunnel. Do you mind me using your picture?"

"Of course not," I said. I had always loved reading books – I never thought I would actually be in one.

"The Hall is a unique building," said Hannah, "but it's the people who have made it really interesting, all through its history."

I thought about this. The first Earl and the secret tunnel... the seventh Earl, mourning his three sons... the tragic story of Frank and Lorna... and other people, dozens of them, including us.

And the story wasn't over. Mallenford Hall was entering a new chapter of its long history. I felt glad we would be there to be part of it.

"Right then," said Mrs Dawkins. "We can't sit here all day. Up you get, girl! Two mirrors done and nine to go!"